The Vienna Trilogy

BOOK ONE

Escape to the West

by Tom Gilligan

Illustrations by Everett Walker

Intelligence e-Publishing Company
Cape Cod, Massachusetts

IEP
Intelligence Book Division

Intelligence e-Publishing Company, Cape Cod, Massachusetts

Illustrations by Everett Walker.

Book Design by Charles King (ckmm.com).

ISBN 978-0-9729659-3-4

Library of Congress Control Number: 2022912940

Contents

For Bonnie

and other wives and children

whose support and sacrifices

helped win the Cold War, 1947–1989.

1

Vienna at Night

**The Date: Tuesday, June 3, 1947—just 24 months after
World War II ended.**

**The Time: Shortly before midnight—when spies go out
for their own "day's work."**

David Hale heard movement on the back stairs. His dad must
be descending to his study, David concluded, when he heard
the fourth creaking sound. Like spies, who work best in the
dark, David was one of the night wanderers of Vienna. He had
already learned well the *nocturnal** sounds of his newest home.
Four months before, within a day of moving into the old castle,
he had made plans for his late night *capers.*† He had scouted
out his new home from *apex*‡ to foundation and, in reverse,
from cellar to tower.

   The first thing David had done was to check out the back
stairs. Creeping upstairs and downward from his second floor
bedroom in several trips, he found three creaky stairs going up
to the attic. He then counted four loose ones going down to

---

*   Nocturnal: Night time.
†   Capers: Adventures.
‡   Apex: The highest point in a structure or building.

the first floor where his dad had his study. Good to know, he figured, when he—or anyone else—moved about the house.

"It'll have to be the tower tonight," David whispered to no one in particular. "The cellar can wait for another time—when the coast is clear and Dad will not hear me."

David had this habit of talking to himself in a barely audible whisper. It made him feel less alone—much like the whistling a person does to *feign confidence** when sensing danger. Before summer passed, David would need every security aid he could *muster.*† By entering the world of *espionage,*‡ his life would be transformed in ways he had never imagined. In fact, he would soon be talking to himself and whistling. But, like a spy, he would be doing it ever so silently.

David was not afraid of the dark. As far back as he could recall, he fought to stay awake at night—not wasting time "going off to lullaby land," as Mom would say when he was a toddler. When David went to bed each night, he felt as if he was going to jail—he saw himself as being no different from a prisoner or caged animal. Some animals prefer daylight—they are called *diurnal.*§ Nocturnal animals, of course, hunt and roam about in the dark. David, however, liked to think of himself as the world's first *biurnal*ⁱ—one of the few persons on the planet who can work and explore day and night.

---

*   Feign confidence: Pretending to appear self assured, safe, and free from danger.
†   Muster: Call forth or rouse.
‡   Espionage: The world of spies where secrets are stolen from other governments.
§   Diurnal: Those that roam about and hunt or eat in the daylight, such as wolves and lions.
ⁱ   Biurnal: David created this word to mean he can operate both in daylight and in the dark.

Sleep! David had reflected on it a great deal and finally calculated that sleep was an enormous waste of time—a waste of life, in fact! "You can't do anything worthwhile in your sleep— except lose half your younger years and a third of your older years." David declared to anyone who would listen when the subject of sleep arose in conversation. Those were the dreadful fractions—one-third and one-half—that David came up with when he first learned to divide. The eight hours most adults sleep divided by the twenty-four-hour day is one-third. The twelve hours little kids sleep divided by the twenty-four-hour day is one-half.

"That's nuts!" he blurted out to Thor, his handsome German shepherd resting peacefully on his rug in the corner. If only David could be like the inventor Thomas Edison, he estimated, the dreadful fraction could be cut down to one-sixth. "Thor, one out of every six hours ought to be the *maximum** time I am forced to lie in bed. Why, if I slept four hours a day, when I am thirty I will have gained five additional years of life. Imagine that!" The dog stared back at David with what the boy considered to be an interested look. But, just as quickly, Thor shut his eyes and dozed back to sleep.

Before *embarking†* on tonight's *trek‡* to the attic, David thought about his dad downstairs in the study. He wondered whether the late evening visit there had anything to do with the startling conversation David had overheard in the afternoon— the talk about gunmen and spies. The spooky conversation had

---

*   Maximum: The most or greatest amount. Opposite of minimum, the least amount.

†   Embarking: Starting or beginning a trip or journey.

‡   Trek: A difficult journey or trip.

occurred shortly before his mom and sister Ellie had left for the airport. They were taking a flight to New York to visit relatives for the summer. David, by choice, was staying in Austria with his dad until late August when they would all meet in New York for a couple of weeks. That was the plan, at least.

His parents' words repeated in David's head. He was excited, certainly—he was *perplexed,** also. After all, his dad was a medical doctor—nothing more. Or, was he still only a doctor?

Dr. Matthew Hale had done secret work during *World War II.*[†] David learned this when his dad returned home from the war after having been reported *missing in action.*[‡] It turned out, in fact, that Matt Hale was not missing at all. Rather, he had been sent into Nazi Germany on a secret intelligence operation. That mission required his medical and German language skills and concerned a group of top German rocket scientists whom the United States Government wished to contact.

David long had wanted his dad to tell him all about the war—especially any secret work he had done. However, since returning safely at war's end, Matt Hale was reluctant to talk about wartime activities. The subject of the war itself, to use one of dad's favorite German words, was *verboten.*[§] "Too many good people died," he said, "for us to be chatting about it idly. Maybe when you get a little older, we can really talk. When it's safe."

---

* Perplexed: Surprised, puzzled, confused by something.
† World War II: The greatest war in history that began in Europe in 1938, spread to Asia in 1941, and affected the whole world before ending in 1945. Sixty million people died in this war.
‡ Missing in action: Being lost in a war and believed to be dead or captured.
§ Verboten: Forbidden, in German.

Due to the afternoon's visit to the study, the boy wanted to go downstairs and ask his father directly about the new secret business. But, if he did, his dad would know that David had *eavesdropped** this afternoon. Listening in on the *cryptic*† remarks of his parents had been unintentional. David knew that. But, he knew also that his being in the study was not entirely *virtuous*‡ either. He was playing *hooky*§ from German class, which surely wouldn't earn him any rewards from his parents. He was in a *quandary.*⁋

David now understood *implicitly*** that things were different from what he had assumed. Vienna was different—his dad was different. And maybe, just maybe, David's own life could be different, too! Or, so he hoped.

He loved his family, the new castle home and faithful Thor, who had an interesting history of his own. In the war, Thor was a U.S. Army *Patrol Dog*†† and was wounded in one of the last battles. "Why, even you, Thor, have had a more exciting life than I've had," David remarked to his *canine*‡‡ pal who showed no interest in the matter. "You may be the best secret keeper of them all, I'm afraid!"

David Hale wanted more in life than growing up *passively*§§

---

*   Eavesdropped: Listened secretly to something that is private.
†   Cryptic: Hidden, mysterious or having a secret meaning.
‡   Virtuous: Innocent or good.
§   Playing hooky: Skipping class or school.
⁋   Quandary: Not knowing what to do.
** Implicitly: To understand naturally without it being pointed out or discussed.
†† Patrol Dog: Dogs used in wartime battles to search out and find enemy soldiers.
‡‡ Canine: The scientific term for dogs.
§§ Passively: Without strong purpose or goals. The opposite of actively.

and *predictably**—"like a mushroom in a cave or a dande-lion in sunlight," he had muttered more than once to Thor. David craved action—something to bring life to his life. *Lo and behold,*† it would happen sooner than he could ever have imagined. He was on the *threshold*‡ of passing into the world of Vienna's spies. This transition would change his life in ways he never expected—boredom would soon be a thing of the past.

---

*   Predictably: Without any surprises or sudden changes.
†   Lo and behold: An expression of surprise on what comes next.
‡   Threshold: The opening or beginning, as a threshold is the entrance-way to a building or home.

2

Why David Hale

David's difficulty in understanding the talk about spies was rather simple—he did not yet grasp what really was going on in Vienna. After all, no one had told him. To this energetic youth, Austria did not seem all that special or interesting. As with an iceberg in the ocean, however, more was going on below the surface than David or most people realized or could see. Spies, naturally, work best when no one has a clue that they are at work—or even around. David soon would learn about mysterious Vienna and about spying itself—from his dad and his new secret life.

It certainly mattered that Vienna, the Austrian *capital city*,* had become the most active *stomping ground*† for spies—more so than far larger cities of the world, including Washington, Moscow, London or Tokyo. What had converted relatively small Vienna into the world's busiest spy center? Geography! Located deep within Eastern Europe, it was wide open to all major nations whose spies flocked there to steal secrets from each other.

But, how did young David Hale come to play an important role in the world of secret intelligence, or espionage? After all,

---

*   Capital city: The City where the government's main offices and officials are located.
†   Stomping ground: Favorite place or territory.

he was eleven years old—"going on twelve," he would quickly add. To begin with, having arrived there in 1947 when things were still *fractured** from the war, he was truly in the right place at the right time. Spies, after all, thrive when things are really messed up, or *chaotic.*† But, Vienna's world of spies was not only because of geography or location. In the late 1940's, many thousands of Americans passed through Vienna and had no connection to the work or the world of spies—at least, none they were aware of!

David, as it would turn out, was a natural for this kind of work. For starters, adventure was in his blood and he was itching for an adventure-filled life. From a young age, he *avidly*‡ read the lives of earlier explorers and heroes—including Alexander the Great, Marco Polo, Daniel Boone, and George Washington. Most of his life's excitement, of course, had come from reading books—Robert Louis Stevenson's "Kidnapped" and James Fenimore Cooper's "The Deerslayer" as well as "The Spy." He read all the Zane Grey books he could get his hands on.

Not only was David Hale curious and full of energy—he also was quite *teachable.*§ When really interested in something, he listened carefully and worked hard to improve his knowledge and sharpen his skills. This was true whether he was building a *slingshot,*⁋ reading a *compass*** and map, or working

---

*   Fractured: Broken apart.

†   Chaotic: When things are completed out of order, messed up, or in what we call chaos.

‡   Avidly: Eagerly or enthusiastically.

§   Teachable: Someone who listens carefully and learns what is being taught.

⁋   Slingshot: A weapon used for hunting that starts with a Y-shaped stick and has rubber bands and a pocket that holds a stone that is shot at great speed.

** Compass: A tool used by sailors, explorers and hikers to find direction and location. It has a thin needle that points northward.

his father's *shortwave radio** to hear broadcasts from around the world, especially from *The States*.†

Most importantly, whenever his dad took time to teach him some subject or skill, he was an eager student. Just being with his dad made him happy—which explains why he begged and pestered his mom to let him stay in Austria for the summer. The three years Dr. Matt Hale had been off to war were the loneliest in David's young life. During the long war, the boy struggled at times to remember his father—how he looked, how he spoke, how it felt when his dad hugged him. Often, David would picture his dad on his way home and being there that very night.

Hundreds of nights came and went, with no Matt Hale coming through the front door. So, David worked his imagination even harder. At such times, he *visualized*‡ his dad as a powerful superhero, such as those in comic books he liked so much. Captain Marvel. Batman. Superman. Well, maybe not as strong as Superman, but pretty close!

Which gets to the final ingredient needed for David's growth into the shadowy world of spies—an excellent teacher. Luckily for David, his teacher would be experienced spy Matt Hale, his favorite man in the whole world. As things would develop, it did not hurt that the master spy would, in turn, require special assistance that only David could provide. An espionage

---

* Shortwave radio: This radio sends signals for hundreds and even thousands of miles and is the favorite of spies who encode their messages so they can only be read by those who have the same code book for decoding messages which means the person receiving the secret message can understand it.

† States: Americans living outside of their country usually call their home "The States," only.

‡ Visualized: Formed a picture in his mind, a mental picture stored in his brain.

partnership was about to be born—a partnering of father and son.

As a result of all four *factors**—having an adventurous spirit, being in the right place when things were really *brewing*,[†] possessing a strong desire to succeed, and having an excellent *mentor*[‡]—David had the potential to grow into a talented spy. A junior spy certainly, but a spy all the same.

When David Hale arrived in Austria less than twenty-four months after the war, Vienna itself was still recovering from the damaging combat that took place during the Battle of Vienna. When the war was over, the armies that defeated Nazi Germany soon *partitioned*[§] Austria into four *sectors*.[¶] Each sector was controlled by one of the four victorious powers—the United States, England, France, and their growing *adversary*,[**] Russia.

Vienna, with one-third of Austria's population, was deep inside the Russian Sector. That was a serious problem because the Russian authorities controlled all of the roads and trains in and out of Vienna. This gave a huge advantage to the Russian military and *spymasters*[††] trying to turn Austria into their ally in an entirely new battle against *The West*.[‡‡] Austria's freedom as an independent nation required huge support from the United

---

*   Factors: The things that make something happen or develop.
†   Brewing: Getting exciting and with a lot of hot things happening.
‡   Mentor: A trusted and very special teacher who guides a person wisely in life.
§   Partitioned: Divided.
¶   Sectors: Parts of a larger system, in this case the country of Austria.
** Adversary: An opponent, foe or enemy.
†† Spymasters: The bosses who are in charge of managing a large number of spies.
‡‡ The West: Meant the free nations that the Russians and Chinese—The East—were fighting to control.

States Government. The aid came in many forms—food, clothing, medicine, as well as money and military equipment.

American spy operations were also needed to block the *subversive** actions of Russian spies who were in Vienna in great numbers. It was in this dangerous setting that young David Hale would begin his career in support of his father's *secret intelligence operations.*† In the end, David Hale's spy operations on the side of freedom would prove to be highly significant— in fact, so important that they were kept "Top Secret" by the U.S. Government for seventy-five years. Until now. Until *"The Vienna Trilogy."*

---

* Subversive: The actions meant to weaken or destroy a free society and people.
† Secret intelligence operations: The work of spies who both steal secrets from enemies and block the actions of an enemy nation's spies.

3

A Spy Again

So, David had learned in the afternoon that his father was back in the spy business—important information he was not supposed to know and could not *readily** talk about. How had David gotten himself into such a pickle? A little before noon that day, he had slipped unnoticed into the study and crawled under dad's massive wooden desk. He had his *whittling†* knife and *sapling‡* branch in hand. His primary goal was to skip the day's lesson in German. He *opted§* to use the time instead to work on making a new slingshot. He thought the flexibility of a fresh tree branch would permit him to shoot much longer distances.

When he heard the study door open, he stayed still. He thought it must be his thirteen-year-old sister Ellie searching for him—the Hale family's extremely *reluctant¶* summer student. With school vacation here, David saw no reason on earth why he should be in school—even for a final German class. Ellie did not need the class and David did not want it.

Instead of it being his sister coming into the study, however, David was surprised to hear his parents talking as they entered

---

*   Readily: Easily or comfortably.
†   Whittling knife: One used to shape wood by cutting off thin pieces.
‡   Sapling branch: Branch from a young tree.
§   Opted: Chose.
¶   Reluctant: Unwilling, not wanting to do something.

the beautiful *wood-paneled** room. Closing the door behind them, his mom and dad believed they were alone.

David's first *inclination*† was to crawl out from under the desk and make his presence known. He certainly was not trying to listen in on anything. But, neither did he have any *zeal*‡ to spend the next ninety minutes in class along with *super-linguist*§ Ellie and German grammar teacher Katrina. They would probably go over vocabulary words for what, to David, seemed the hundredth time. There was also the probability Katrina would drill him repeatedly on his pronunciation, which was improving but not as good as Ellie's.

Already beginning to sound like an Austrian *fräulein*,¶ she would sit in class with a gleeful twinkle in her eyes as David struggled to pronounce new German words correctly. "I'll bet she can't use a slingshot," he *mused*,** "or climb to the castle tower without making a single sound. Or pick up a snake."

After the door was closed and locked, his mom spoke in a soft but determined voice. "Matt, the war has been over for two years! When millions were fighting and dying all around the world, it was one thing. You now have important medical work to do—leave the Russian problem to professional spies. I am proud of what you did in the war. Right now, however, I want a normal life for our family—and a safe one."

---

*   Wood-paneled: Having nice wood on the walls of a room.
†   Inclination: A natural tendency in a certain direction.
‡   Zeal: Strong interest in doing something.
§   Super-linguist: A person who is really good at learning and speaking foreign languages.
¶   Fräulein: German word for young girl.
** Mused: To think deeply about something.

David was dazed by what he was hearing. His *respiration**
changed. The more he tried to control or calm his breathing,
the deeper each breath became. And, when Matt Hale walked
around to the rear of the desk, David could practically touch
his father's shoes. So, the youth's heavy breathing worsened
even more.

He knew, too, that if dad sat down he would be discovered—the family spy hiding in the *recesses†* of the old desk. In
the least, he would be sent scurrying off to German class. At
worst, they would be upset if they thought David had been
purposely listening in on their private talk. It was now too
late for an *honorable‡* exit. And, it was too late not to hear the
intriguing§ business about spies. So, David figured, maybe it
would help if he tried not to hear any more.

He placed the knife and emerging slingshot on the rug.
Then, he reached up slowly and placed a hand over each ear. In
that way, if discovered, David in all honesty could say he tried
not to listen. He covered his ears for several minutes. He now
heard only *muffled¶* sounds of his parents' voices—nothing he
could *comprehend.*** For the moment, he felt safe. Well, if not
entirely safe, at least safer. All the while, he watched his father
from the knees of his pants downward, pacing back and forth.

Then David's own body betrayed him—his nose began to
itch. He tried ignoring it at first by thinking of other things; for

---

* Respiration: Breathing.
† Recesses: Hidden part of something—usually deep inside.
‡ Honorable: Noble, good, virtuous or worthy of praise.
§ Intriguing: Fascinating or exciting—involving mystery.
¶ Muffled: Not able to be heard because something is blocking the
  sound.
** Comprehend: Understand.

example, running in the park with Thor or shooting at small targets with his slingshot. Nothing helped. The bridge of his nose got itchier and itchier. He wrinkled his face with all the might of his facial muscles. He wiggled his nose like a rabbit. Nothing worked! The itch only got worse.

He felt like screaming out because the unscratched itch had become unbearable. Despite *misgivings** about again listening in on his parents, he removed his right hand from his ear. He slowly *maneuvered*† it to the front of his face in the direction of the itch. All the while, he prayed his dad would not sit down. To his surprise, David quickly found that one uncovered ear was about as good as two ears when it came to eavesdropping.

Now, he clearly heard his dad speaking. "As I said already, dear, I did not volunteer for anything. They asked if I would provide a little special assistance—no shooting this time, so no one should get hurt. They said the Russians are less reckless these days—now that three of their own gunmen have disappeared."

David reached the itchy spot and scratched ever so slowly. The relief was *exhilarating*.‡ His hand shot back up to his right ear and the parents' conversation became *unintelligible*§ again. After a few minutes passed, both parents left the study before David slipped out and climbed up the back stairs to his room. As he made his silent ascent, he heard Ellie in the kitchen speaking German as only she could after a few months of study.

---

*   Misgivings: Feeling of doubt about something.
†   Maneuvered: A careful movement.
‡   Exhilarating: To become very happy or cheerful.
§   Unintelligible: Unclear and not able to be understood.

His thoughts were not on his *sibling** or German class, however. Instead, his head *reeled*† over what he had just heard—"Spies! Russians! Gunmen!"

---

*   Sibling: Brother or sister.
†   Reeled: Spun or went around and around.

4

Stairwell Acrobatics

The Date: Wednesday, June 4, 1947

The Time: 12:00AM

As the chimes in the hall sounded midnight, David glided quietly across the floor of his room in stocking feet. He moved diagonally toward the front left window and around the creaky flooring which had tripped him up the first night in the castle. Stepping on those loose boards had alerted the family *sentinel*** Ellie that David was roaming about the large house. She did her usual, big-sister thing and called out loudly so all could hear that David was, as she put it, on the prowl.

"What a pain!" he thought at the time—but only briefly. Because David changed his *tactics,*† she had not caught him in weeks. *Ironically*‡ as well as unintentionally, his big sister had become his ally. How? When she did NOT call out in the night, everyone assumed David must be securely in bed. In the language of spies, this now gave him the *cover*§ he needed for

---

*   Sentinel: A guard or sentry who protects things.
†   Tactics: The planned and disciplined way of doing something that re-quires skills.
‡   Ironically: When something unexpected or opposite happens.
§   Cover: Cover is the innocent-looking action or explanation that hides the real spy action taking place. For example, a spy looks like he has gone shopping but he really is placing a signal on a wall with chalk.

undetected nighttime exploration of the castle's chambers and passageways, as well as its countless *nooks and crannies*.*

Weeks earlier, Ellie had assisted David's nightly explorations in another unintended way. For his birthday, she gave him what became a valuable aid for exploring in the dark—a U.S. Army flashlight with six batteries. The foot-long *tubular device*† enabled him to look through old trunks and closets without turning on any overhead lights.

When he used the powerful flashlight without any covering, it *emitted*‡ a beam that seemed sunlight bright. When he needed to be more secretive, he could reduce the glow *appreciably*§ by putting a light sock over the flashlight. To expose even less light, he used a green German Army sock with a small hole in the toe. He found it in the cellar along with some other military stuff, including maps and helmets.

The flashlight and two socks became, as he called them, his trusty trio. He stored the trio in his own secret hiding place—beneath a loose floor board he found in the closet of his bedroom. Before long, David would hide more important things there, things of value and of interest to spies.

David reached the hallway and *hooked*¶ a right onto the first stair. This one was solid and gave no hint that David was up and about. The next two stairs gave off no sound unless he pressed

---

* Nooks and crannies: Little places and hiding areas such as underneath stairs or deep parts of closets.
† Tubular device: A tool which is shaped like a tube.
‡ Emitted: To come out of; for example, the sun emits light or a horn emits a sound.
§ Appreciably: A great deal, quite a lot, considerably.
¶ Hooked a right: Made a circular turn onto the stairs, in the shape of a hook used in fishing.

down too hard. So, he pulled with both arms on the *banister**
to support some of his weight. Then came tricky stairs four and
five, each sure to produce a *telltale†* noise if David so much as
lightly touched either one with his foot.

At first, the technique for *scaling‡* the two stairs was awk-
ward, even difficult. However, he practiced his stair climbing
and, within days, had become very good. He would reach up
and grab the railing with both hands and place his left foot on
the wooden *molding§* that ran alongside the stairs. He pulled
himself up forcefully and slid two feet until he was able to place
his right foot onto stair number six.

At this point in his climb, he was off-balance. He had to
kneel onto stair seven, first with his right knee and then his
left. At this point, he could stand up and walk again toward the
summit.¶ "This is not exactly *Mount Everest,*** *Mount McKinley,††*
or the *Matterhorn,*‡‡" he thought, "but the best thing available
at the moment."

At stair thirteen, he again had to be cautious. He could put
some weight onto the right half of the stair without making

---

*   Bannister: The hand railing in a stair case that keeps a person from
    falling.
†   Telltale: An outward sign or warning.
‡   Scaling: Climbing up and over some barrier; for example over a cliff
    or mountain.
§   Molding: Fancy wood used for decoration around windows and along
    stairways.
¶   Summit: The highest point or top of something—such as a mountain.
** Mount Everest: Highest Mountain in the world is in Asia: 29,028 feet,
    or almost 6 miles high.
†† Mount McKinley: Highest Mountain in North America is in Canada,
    20,320 feet, and 4 miles high.
‡‡ Matterhorn: Beautiful Mountain in Switzerland climbed by only the
    best mountain climbers.

a sound. But, any downward force to the left of center would surely make a noise and end his escape. It happened the third night in the castle when David developed his peculiar case of *triskai-deca-stepa-phobia**—his own created word for fear of stair thirteen. It was at that point in his ascent that Ellie detected him—ending the night's flight to freedom when she sounded the alarm. But, that was the last time he had been caught.

Now, with his sister on her way to New York, David found that he actually missed having a sentinel he could fool. Her absence took much of the challenge—and fun—out of *clandestine*† exploration.

Reaching the final stair, David waited a few seconds, letting his eyes get used to the castle's dark *garret*.‡ He moved quickly into the first chamber on the right. *Blackout curtains*§ left over from the war covered the windows. *Scant*⁋ light came in, even on the brightest of nights. Tonight, there was a full moon. Compared to his earlier homes, the castle at first seemed creepy. Now, David was accustomed to moving about quietly in the dark.

For one thing, the cobwebs that *invariably*** caught his face no longer bothered him—once he learned that Austria had no

---

*   Triskai-deca-<u>stepa</u>-phobia: Triskaidekaphobia is fear of the number 13; David fears step #13.

†   Clandestine: Something done in secrecy so that no one else knows what is happening.

‡   Garret: The attic area just below the roof of the castle.

§   Blackout curtains: Dark black shades or curtains to keep inside lights from being seen from outside.

⁋   Scant: Very little.

**   Invariably: Not changing, always, consistently.

deadly spiders. What David had yet to realize, though, was that the previous occupants were worse than the worst of poisonous spiders. Nazis had walked the castle halls planning and committing crimes of every sort against freedom-loving Austrians. For almost seven years, it had been a "center of evil." In time, Dr. Matt and David Hale would cleanse that terrible stain by turning the castle into a *haven** of hope and freedom—although a very secret one.

---

* Haven: A place of safety or refuge—often called a safe haven.

5

The Midnight Visitor

The young *sleuth** drifted over to the first window and peered down at the garden below. *Stratus clouds†* *obscured‡* light from the moon but, generally, the rear garden seemed quite bright. Light from his dad's study—partially blocked by thick bushes that *nestled§* around the castle—was barely visible. As David glanced about the garden, he spotted movement near the study. A human figure flashed past the window, then cut across the lawn away from the house and, finally, continued in the direction of the pathway leading down to the river.

Hairs on the young night wanderer's head and neck came alive and seemed to stand on end. David's next sensation was a chill running down his spine. Clearly, he was scared. He worried not for himself, though, but for his father. Was his dad okay? Who was the *furtive§* stranger? Had Dr. Hale spotted him, too? With questions but no answers, David immediately *resolved*** to slip downstairs to see what was occurring—and of course make sure his dad was all right.

---

* Sleuth: Detective or person that uncovers secrets.
† Stratus clouds: Flat, stretched clouds usually found between 2,000 and 7,000 feet in the air.
‡ Obscured: Hid or partly blocked.
§ Nestled: Hugged or comfortably rested—as in, "the children all nestled asleep in their beds."
§ Furtive: Acting secretly as though one has something to hide.
** Resolved: Made a firm decision.

David *retraced** his earlier journey to the garret. With the instinct of a *predator,*† he made his way *adroitly*‡ down the attic stairs to the second floor. Stair thirteen posed little problem as David, this time, used the left side of the staircase to support his weight. Stairs four and five were easily avoided in the descent as his foot—with the help of gravity—slid effortlessly down the wooden molding. With help of the banister, he reduced the downward pressure on stairs two and three.

He used the tricks of his practiced routine to get to the first floor—this time *eluding*§ four squeaky stairs on the way. Thanks to his training and practice, his anxiety to find his dad did not interfere with his agility. He descended from the garret to second floor and on to the first floor in less than seven seconds—without making a sound. *Disciplined*⁋ practice worked, after all. A panther in the jungle or a wolf pack on the hunt all move about their own *turf*** with remarkably similar stealth.

Reaching the study, David saw his dad working calmly at his desk where the boy had hidden earlier in the day. David felt tremendous relief. "Someone's out in the garden, Dad. I saw a big guy dashing into the woods, heading for the river," he exclaimed.

For a brief *interval,*†† Matt Hale looked at his son, *grimaced,*‡‡ and told David to sit down so they might have a brief chat.

---

*   Retraced: Go in the opposite way or direction.
†   Predator: An animal that hunts or preys on other animals.
‡   Adroitly: Skillfully or cleverly.
§   Eluding: Skillfully avoiding; like the mice eluded the trap set to catch them.
⁋   Disciplined: Hard work that made him a skilled staircase acrobat.
** Turf: The land where an animal roams around.
†† Interval: Period of time between two events or happenings.
‡‡ Grimaced: Twisted his face in a way that showed he was annoyed.

"Son, that 'big guy' was visiting me. But, I am curious—how could you possibly see the garden from your bedroom—on the other side of the castle? Unless, of course, you were prowling in the upper chambers again."

David wondered how his dad correctly concluded that he may have been in the garret. Had he known all along about David's middle-of-the-night trips? The young fellow at first was stunned—then he was embarrassed.

Hoping to change the subject—and take attention off his own secret movements—he said, "I was wide awake, Dad. Was out exploring. Found some neat German medals and military stuff I'd like to show you, when you have some time."

His father spoke not a word, but continued to stare at him. So, David tried to avoid answering by, instead, asking his own questions. "Who visited you at midnight, Dad? Why would he leave through the rear garden and the river—not through the front entrance and the roadway?"

For a moment, Matt Hale hesitated and then spoke slowly in a serious tone. "Son, there are some specific things we can discuss later—not tonight. It's late. But, from our chats, you should know that a major struggle is *underway** here in Austria. In fact, all across Europe. No one knows whether the Russians will take over Austria—just as they already have taken over most of Eastern Europe. Russia's powerful *Red Army*† is certainly strong enough to do it. I am hearing that the Russians, in fact, will be in full control of neighboring Czechoslovakia in

---

*   Underway: Happening or taking place.
†   Red Army: Red is the chosen color for Communism.

a matter of months. So, Son, if they *prevail** here in Vienna—
and if they eventually control all of Western Europe—the very
freedoms so many fought and died for in World War II will be
entirely lost."

His dad continued. "*Communism*[†] is a very poor substitute
for the murderous system of the Nazis. 'Visitor' is working to
ensure[‡] that the Russians do not succeed. I have been asked—
and have agreed—to give him a hand. Without *elaborating*[§]
right now, I may need some help. You can start by keeping
tonight's discussion—and 'Visitor"s being here confidential.
Between us, only! No mention of this to Ellie in any short
wave messages or letters. Nor can you speak about any of this
to Katrina or her husband. They're good people—but, they
have no *need to know*."[¶]

David's eyes widened—he was about to ask a *slew*** of
questions when his dad whisked him out of the study. The
doctor-spy repeated to him that the middle of the night was
no time to talk. "By the way, son, please *refrain from*[††] whittling
under my desk. I have a hard enough time keeping the study

---

* Prevail: Win or gain victory.
† Communism: An evil system of government that takes freedoms away
  from the citizens and gives all important decision making and power
  to a small unelected group—The Communist Party. Communist
  Governments in Russia, China, North Korea and Cuba have killed
  more than one hundred million people in the past hundred years.
  Most of the murder victims were their own citizens!
‡ Ensure: To guarantee or make happen.
§ Elaborating: Telling all of the facts.
¶ Need to know: This is one of the most important or basic rules in the
  world of spies—you tell someone only what he or she must know to
  do an intelligence operation.
** Slew: A large number.
†† Refrain from: Stop doing something.

clean." The remark caught David by surprise—but his dad's smile, before sending him upstairs, reassured him he was not in trouble.

The final surprise of the evening came when Matt Hale winked and said, "Be careful with stairs three, five, seven and twelve on the way to your room—don't want to awaken the castle goblins." Then and there, he *grasped** the reality that his dad was more aware than he had imagined—about Austria, about the castle and about David himself. As he entered his room, Thor looked up and wagged his tail. Suspiciously, David stared at his *lethargic*† pet and wondered whether Thor too might have secrets he wasn't revealing. "Naw, my imagination is running wild from all this spy stuff," he murmured. "Have to settle down."

David Hale lay wide awake for another hour, recalling the day's events. He could hardly wait until dawn—once the sun came up, no one would keep him in bed.

---

* Grasped: Understood immediately.
† Lethargic: Lazy, without energy, tired.

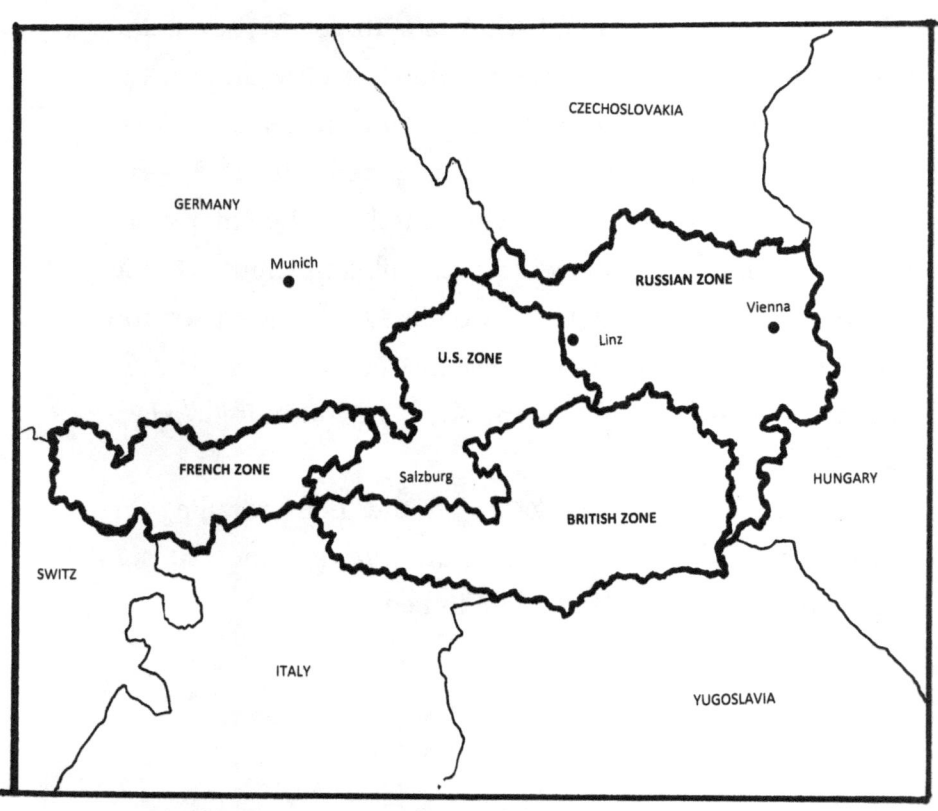

CZECHOSLOVAKIA

GERMANY

Munich

RUSSIAN ZONE

Vienna

U.S. ZONE

Linz

FRENCH ZONE

Salzburg

BRITISH ZONE

HUNGARY

SWITZ

ITALY

YUGOSLAVIA

6

The Russians Are Here

The Date: Wednesday, June 4, 1947.

The Time: 8:00AM

Instead of rising before sunrise as usual, however, David slept late—until well after the roosters stopped crowing down at the chicken coop. When he did awaken, he jumped out of bed, threw on his clothes and ran down the corridor to his dad's room. Not finding him there, he headed for the kitchen.

Matt Hale was having Turkish coffee, which was popular in Vienna's old coffee houses. Thor, on the floor next to dad, was getting a back rub. In the war, the old Patrol Dog was hit by a bullet that left him with some muscle damage and stiffness. He never grew tired of a good *massage*.*

"Hey, Dad, a good time to have that talk?"

"Sure, son, let's take a walk—but, first, grab yourself a little breakfast. Thor has had his fill."

David had a quick breakfast and the two strolled out through the kitchen door, with Matt Hale in the lead. They headed in the direction of the river. They could see Katrina working in the garden next to her cottage at the entrance to the castle grounds.

---

*   Massage: Rubbing sore, damaged or stiff muscles to reduce pain and improve recovery.

She was planting seedlings for vegetables because food was scarce and prices had *soared** in the post-war period. This was an unfortunate result from the fact that most of Austria's farms were in the east—in the Russian Sector.

After the war, from mid-1945 through mid-1947, the Americans had been bringing *massive*[†] amounts of food into the country to feed both Austrians as well as the tens of thousands of *Displaced Persons*[‡] in the camps for *refugees.*[§] While the Americans brought in food, the Russians were doing the opposite—they were stealing Austrian-grown food and sending it out of the country and on to Russia.

The Russians were doing the same thing with the machinery and *heavy equipment*[ⁱ] which they stole from the factories in their sector of Austria—that too was shipped out of Austria and on to Russia. *In light of all this,*[**] Matt Hale would comment, only *half in jest,*[††] "Countries that lose a war to Russia will starve, lose their warm clothing—and even be left without toilets."

When they reached the river bank, Matt Hale sat on a log and waited until David was equally settled and ready to chat. He looked down at his son and said "Look, sorry I cut you off last night—I had to do some planning and thinking about how to

---

*   Soared: Rose or increased to a very high level.

†   Massive: Great or enormous quantities.

‡   Displaced Persons: Also called, D.P.'s for short, these were the hundreds of thousands of refugees mainly from Eastern Europe who did not want to return to their home countries that had been taken over by the Communists and the Russian Army.

§   Refugees: People who left or were thrown out of their country during war and have no country of their own.

ⁱ   Heavy equipment: Tractors, plows, railroad engines and cars, automobiles and trucks.

**   In light of this: Because of this.

††   Half in jest: In sort of a funny way, but really a serious matter.

go about a rescue operation. I have to help a man escape from the Russian Sector—very soon, or it could be too late for him. Before discussing *how* this might be done, let's take some time and talk about *why* this must be done. After all, the *why* tells us how important or *crucial** it is to take risks to get this man out of the Russian Sector and to freedom."

"I know why I agreed to help—I want you to understand as well. To begin with, let's be sure you don't think the intelligence or spy business is some sort of game—just a fun thing to do. It is, in fact, serious and *critically*† important. Can we agree on that?"

"Sure thing, Dad!" was David's instant response. He was already beginning to feel he was on his Dad's team.

Matt Hale continued. "There are things about this you need to *comprehend*‡ as clearly as any adult can. *Maturity*§ comes to different individuals at different ages. I am confident you are both serious and grown up enough to handle this information. I have seen too many adults in my life who continue to act and think like children—they get stuck more or less as lifelong *adolescents*."¶ They make very poor doctors and equally bad spies.

"By contrast, in the war, I saw *firsthand*** that boys your age grasped what was *at stake*†† and did very brave things when their

---

* Crucial: How important or urgent something is.
† Critically: Severely or dangerously urgent.
‡ Comprehend: Understand and to know.
§ Maturity: How serious and responsible a person is—the opposite of childishness.
¶ Adolescents: The time between childhood and adulthood.
** Firsthand: Directly and in person—not merely from the gossip or reports of other people.
†† What is at stake: The importance of something.

country was attacked. Many Polish youngsters at the time even fought the foreign *invaders**—first, the Nazis from the west and, then, the Russians from the east. Unfortunately, Poland was caught between two armies of invading *barbarians*.[†] But, for starters, let's talk about Austria, and specifically Vienna. Do you know why this city is so important?"

Initially, David was at a loss for words. He was accustomed to being asked history questions by his mom—not his dad. David thought a moment and said the first thing that came into his mind. "Don't know a lot about Vienna yet, Dad. But, I am curious—we were once an ally of the Russians and that was only a couple of years ago. Why are we against each other now?"

Matt looked at David and responded carefully. "Excellent question—one that is important as well as complex. Without turning this into a boring history class, let me explain. You're a little sick of school, I hear. Well, I will have to back up a bit, Son, and cover some recent history—things that led up to the war itself."

"Yes, the United States and the British started helping the Russians. That was in 1941, after they were attacked by Nazi Germany. Ours was an *alliance of convenience*[‡]—it did not mean the Russian Communists had become our permanent ally, much less great friends. Only two years earlier, these same

---

* Invaders: Those armies that attack other countries.
† Barbarians: A brutal uncivilized people who act cruelly and without a sense of decency.
‡ Alliance of convenience: A partnership between countries that was useful in practical terms but not because the nations had the same ideas about how people should be treated and governed.

Russians partnered with Hitler and the Nazis in a secret *pact**
or deal to conquer peaceful Poland and divide that country and
most of Eastern Europe between them!"

"Only because Hitler was the greater evil and threat to
America and England in the war, did we decide to support
Russia. Was it because we trusted them? Not at all! Rather, it
was the surest and quickest way to defeat the Nazis and win a
war that, if we lost it, would have cost all of us our freedoms."

"How could we be certain that Russia never became our true
partner? It gets back to spying—our secret agents in Russia
reported in 1943 that Russia's Communist leader, *Joseph Stalin,*[†]
had told his intelligence organizations that America was Russia's
main enemy[‡]—'*glavni vrag*' is the Russian term for it. Stalin gave
orders to his spies to go after America at the time we Americans
were sending Russia thousands of shipments of military equipment as well as food and clothing! So, it is absolutely certain
that we never had a true partner in the Russians."

"Time after time, they have shown themselves willing to
betray allies and break agreements whenever it is in their interest to do so. The Red Army repeatedly showed they had no
interest in liberating or truly freeing other countries from Nazi
control. Instead, their plan was and is to turn the countries of
Europe into Communist nations and destroy their freedoms."

---

*   Pact: An agreement between nations to work together as allies.

†   Joseph Stalin: The evil leader of Soviet Russia for more than twenty
years. The number of people he had murdered is somewhere around
forty million—making him one of the greatest killers in human
history.

‡   Main Enemy: The Russian term is *glavni vrag*. This meant that, while
Stalin was supposedly an ally of the United States, he was secretly call-
ing America the most important enemy of Soviet Russia.

David listened *intently** to all that his father was saying. He then returned to the first subject his dad had raised earlier: "What about Vienna, Dad? Why is this place so important?"

Matt smiled, impressed that David was asking the most *immediate*[†] question. After all, it was just outside Vienna where he faced the challenge of rescuing a person from the Russian Secret Police. This rescue operation would take place in Austria's Russian Sector where the Russian Army and Secret Police controlled much of the *landscape*[‡] and all the means of *transportation*.[§] It was also where Russian kidnappings and murders had recently become an *epidemic*[¶] of sorts.

Matt Hale responded. "VIENNA! This is indeed an important place. It is a *strategic*[**] city—it has been one since the ancient Romans built a military camp and fortress here to protect themselves from Germanic tribes to their north. That was 2,000 years ago! The Romans stayed here for five hundred years—until Rome itself fell to Germanic invaders who effectively ended one of the great empires in human history."

He continued: "Ever since, Vienna has been a key *crossroads*[††] in European history. After all, one of the world's great waterways—the Danube River—flows through Vienna and ten countries on its eighteen hundred mile journey. It runs from

---

*   Intently: With great interest and seriousness.
†   Immediate: The first matter of importance or timing.
‡   Landscape: The physical geography of roads and highways, hills and valleys.
§   Means of transportation: The trains, bridges, airports, and highways in and out of Vienna.
¶   Epidemic: A bad disease affecting a population or region at the same time.
** Strategic: Of great importance to plans and goals.
†† Crossroads: A place where great roads from many lands meet

high in the Black Forest of Germany down to the Black Sea
that separates Europe from Asia."

"And, Son, the Russians—who are among the best *chess**
players in the world—know the strategic value of Vienna. In
March 1945, the Red Army captured the city—they have no
intention now of just walking away from what they consider
theirs. They see Vienna as a place where their spies can steal
lots of secrets from lots of nations."

Matt Hale waited a bit till this information sunk in and
David had a little time to think about things he was hearing
for the first time—the things of spies.

"My job," he continued, "is to do something that would
be extremely difficult for American intelligence officers to do.
American officials drive cars with US Government markings on
them—my car does not! They are known to the Russians who
suspect all of them to be spies. Instead, the Russians probably
see me as merely a doctor trying to stop the spread of deadly
typhus† around the refugee camps. They probably think I am
too busy fighting disease to be working also as a spy. That is
our *ace in the hole*‡—our advantage."

Father and son finished their chat and headed back up the
hill to the castle. Matt Hale told David to remember the "need-
to-know" principle—the boy must *refrain*§ from discussing
these things with anyone else. "Right now, I've got some work

---

* Chess: A board game that requires great skill and thinking several
  moves ahead.
† Typhus: A deadly disease spread by lice bites that infect people living
  in overcrowded camps.
‡ Ace in the hole: Edge or advantage—as in poker where the aces have
  the highest value.
§ Refrain from: Hold one back from doing something.

to do in the study. Maybe we can play *cribbage** after dinner. Better still, since we're going against the Russians, maybe we should play some chess."

David gave a wide smile—he loved playing his dad in games of any kind. Except for shooting a slingshot, the youngster lost to his dad much of the time—but his attitude was "So what! Dad's all mine when we're playing anything."

*   Cribbage: A card game played usually by two people and using a board to keep score.

7

Ping, Ping, Ping

The Date: Thursday, June 5, 1947

The Time: 6:45AM

Early the next morning, Dr. Matt Hale was back at his desk in the study when David took Thor out to the garden for exercise and for a little target practice with the newest home-made sling-shot. This was not the *excessively** flexible one he had whittled while hiding under his father's oak desk. That one, it turned out, did indeed shoot rocks and *horse chestnuts*[†] an extremely long distance.

David discovered, however, that the *whippyness*[‡] of the sap-ling branch made his shooting far less accurate. With slingshots, David was learning, it was most important to hit what he was aiming at—in fact, the single most important quality of a good slingshot is its *accuracy*.[§] Having learned this lesson, he had whittled yet another slingshot but, this time, from a *sturdy*[¶] branch.

---

* Excessively: More than is necessary or wanted.
† Horse chestnuts: They look like other chestnuts but are poisonous to humans.
‡ Whippyness: Like a whip, the ability of the material to snap back after it is bent or pulled.
§ Accuracy: The ability to hit a target time after time.
¶ Sturdy: Solid, stronger and less whippy.

As Dr. Matt Hale tried to concentrate on the problem at hand, the sounds "ping, ping, ping" drifted through the open window. David was shooting pebbles at empty Coca Cola bottles resting on top of the garden wall. More often than not, he wasn't missing as this was the best shooting device he had yet whittled. Its accuracy was clear from the *incessant** sounds of stone striking glass—ping–ping–ping. Satisfied with the results he was getting with his new device, the younger Hale was feeling pretty good.

"Ten in a row! Fifteen in a row! I wonder whether anyone has ever shot a hundred straight." All this was going through the boy's mind as he went about his practice.

Matt Hale, *on the contrary,*[†] was becoming annoyed that his son had picked that spot and that time to target practice. It made it harder for him to focus on the secret mission which could turn out to be *exceedingly*[‡] difficult, mainly because it had to be carried out so soon. But, whether in a hurry or not, his operational planning still had to be *flawless.*[§] Any mistake in timing or performance could cost a good man his freedom—permanently!

'Visitor' had *outlined*[¶] the problem *succinctly***—an important scientist had to be *evacuated*[††] secretly from the Russian Sector in Austria—the sooner the better! The urgent and risky assignment was given to the person with the best chance to

---

*   Incessant: Unending, not stopping.
†   On the contrary: Quite the opposite.
‡   Exceedingly: Very.
§   Flawless: Without any mistakes or errors—foolproof.
¶   Outlined: Described generally without all of the details.
** Succinctly: Briefly and to the point.
††   Evacuated: Removed or taken away from.

accomplish the operation—Dr. Matthew Hale. In his medical work in the refugee camps and in the hospitals surrounding Vienna, he was *uniquely** able to move about more or less freely. And, he knew very well the streets in the Russian Sector where he would have to rescue the scientist.

Like all Western travelers, Matt Hale was at times *harassed*† by Russian Border Guards—at other times, even by the murderous Russian Secret Police. But, his medical work gave him the *justification*‡ needed to drive from sector to sector throughout Austria. That, in turn, would give him also the operational cover to do secret intelligence tasks with less risk of being detected.

American Intelligence§ officials had learned from a recently-arrived refugee that a famous Polish scientist, Dr. Stanislaw Kaminski, was hiding in the Russian Sector under a *false identity*.¶ The refugee reported that Dr. Kaminski wanted to go to the United States to continue his *nuclear research*.** His specific field of expertise—nuclear safety—was important in medical research, nuclear power plants and in building nuclear bombs. If the Russians found him, he knew, they would certainly make him work in building bombs. But, Kaminski was tired of war. It was *vital*†† that he be moved out of Austria before the Russian Secret Police discovered his real identity

---

*   Uniquely: Being the only one.
†   Harassed: Bothered, disturbed or hassled.
‡   Justification: A good reason for doing something.
§   American Intelligence: The spy organization that worked against the Nazis and then the Russians.
¶   False identity: Using a name different from one's real name.
** Nuclear research: Studying what is possible in the field of atomic energy. This includes everything from making bombs to finding ways to fight cancer.
†† Vital: Extremely important.

and location. If they did, they would *kidnap** him and send him off to Russia—or kill him if he gave them too much trouble.

Since the war, hundreds of scientists—as well as hundreds of thousands of Eastern European refugees and *prisoners of war*[†]—had been *spirited*[‡] off to Russia. Tens of thousands never returned to their homeland—nor were they seen or heard from again. Why did the Russians want all these foreign prisoners?

Back during the war, a half million of Russia's own *forced laborers*[§] died in *Siberia*[¶] from overwork, freezing temperatures as well as from starvation and beatings. To replace the dead Russian prisoners, the Russian Government decided to kidnap German and other prisoners of war—as well as simple homeless refugees—not letting them leave Siberia for their own countries when the war was over.

Laborers** were sent to mines and forests where, again, hundreds of thousands of them were worked to death in terribly harsh conditions. The Communist authorities did not care when these uneducated people were killed by their Secret Police or died in other ways. As far as they were concerned, that was how their system of *terror*[††] worked best.

---

*   Kidnap: To take a person away by force.

[†]   Prisoners of war: These were foreign soldiers captured by the Soviet Red Army.

[‡]   Spirited off: To make people disappear mysteriously—as though by ghosts.

[§]   Forced laborers: These were prisoners sent by the Communists to work camps—for life!

[¶]   Siberia: The huge northern part of Russia that is mainly cold, forested and lonely and where Communist Governments sent millions of political prisoners to be worked to death in mining and tree cutting.

**   Laborers: Men who work with their hands building roads, bridges and tunnels as well as cutting trees.

[††]   Terror: The use of murder and violence to make people so scared that they do what they are told.

Scientists, however, were extremely valuable to the Russians, and they were sent to research centers near Russia's capital, Moscow. Most of these educated and highly trained experts were forced to work in military weapons programs.

So far, Dr. Kaminski had barely avoided being captured within the Russian Sector. He now believed it was only a matter of days before his true identity would be discovered by the Russians. So, he asked his refugee friend to contact the Americans. He saw this as his very last chance to escape.

In Poland, after the war, Dr. Kaminski saw that living under Communism was little different from living under the Nazis. In each case, there were none of the freedoms available in Poland before the war or now in the West. He was aware also that the Russian Secret Police had murdered more than 20,000 Polish prisoners of war. The secret executions took place in 1940 in the Katyn Forest, a short distance from the city of Smolensk in Soviet Russia. Kaminski personally knew many of these victims from his own student and teaching days in the university.

Why did Russia's Secret Police *execute*[*] so many of Poland's military officers and educated leaders? The reason was *political*[†]—after the killings, it would be easier for Russia to turn Poland into part of the growing Communist empire. By these *brutal*[‡] acts of murder, the Russian Communists were making sure that, at war's end, many of the leading Polish opponents of Communism would already be dead.

---

[*]   Executed: Murdered or killed on orders—in this case, from the Soviet Government in Moscow.
[†]   Political: For reasons of government power and control, in this case of the Polish population.
[‡]   Brutal: Cruel, barbaric, evil.

Matt Hale's first task tomorrow was to get a message to Kaminski. Escape instructions had to be delivered to him without alerting the Russians. Matt Hale could not risk having a *face-to-face** meeting with the Polish scientist before the escape itself. That would be dangerous. If the Secret Police—or any of their *informants*†—saw Dr. Kaminski meeting with a foreigner, especially an American, they would investigate and quickly discover the scientist's *true identity.*‡

Neither could Matt Hale make a simple telephone call to contact Dr. Kaminski. The Russians *tapped*§ the phone lines in all of Vienna—any phone call could *endanger*⁋ the scientist and lead to his arrest. A basic rule for every spy—do not use telephones to make contact—instead, find another safer way!

Initially,** Matt Hale thought about doing a night-time *black pajama operation*†† to get the escape plan to Dr. Kaminski. In such a *ploy,*‡‡ the doctor-spy would dress in dark clothing and sneak on foot into the Russian Sector. However, the full moon this week was too bright for that. With so much moonlight, it would be too risky to try to move *surreptitiously*§§ on foot around the Russian Sector—he might be spotted by Russian Border

---

*   Face to face meeting: When two people meet personally, not by telephone for example.

†   Informants: People who work secretly for the police in Communist and Nazi countries and report on other citizens—especially on those who would like to escape.

‡   True identity: Who a person really is.

§   Tapped: Secretly listening in on the telephone calls of other people.

⁋   Endanger: To place in a risky or dangerous situation.

**   Initially: At first or in the beginning.

††   Black Pajama Operation: Dressing entirely in black clothes to be able to sneak around in the dark of night without being seen.

‡‡   Ploy: A trick, move or action designed to fool an opponent or enemy to gain advantage.

§§   Surreptitiously: Sneaking around without being seen.

Guards. The *new moon** that gives off little light would not be for another two weeks—on June 18. But, with the Russians *screening*† refugees more carefully these days, Kaminski could be arrested by then. Another way had to be found!

While Matt Hale studied his street map of the Austrian Russian Sector, he couldn't ignore the *vexing*‡ sounds as David continued shooting at Coke bottles. Finding it hard to think through the rescue operation while his son ping–ping–ping'd in the garden, Matt Hale was ready to *dispatch*§ David to another part of the castle grounds. Then, like a bolt of lightning, it struck him. The message could be delivered *airborne*¶ after all—by slingshot! In a heartbeat, ping–ping–ping took on the air of a *sonata.*** Instantly, the irritating noise of stones hitting glass had been transformed into *melody.*††

Matt Hale bounded out the study door and into the garden. He exclaimed, "David, it's time we work on our *joint venture.*‡‡ We're going for a ride—bring your slingshot and plenty of *ammo.*§§ Horse chestnuts will be just fine." A partnership in *clandestinity*¶¶ was born—senior-spy needed junior-spy. As they

---

*   New Moon: Unlike a bright Full Moon, the New Moon gives off little light—a good time to sneak across borders between countries because the Border Guards cannot see you.
†   Screening: Carefully examining identity papers by police.
‡   Vexing: Bothersome. Irritating or distracting.
§   Dispatch: To send away.
¶   Airborne: Through the air.
** Sonata: A musical piece written for instruments.
†† Melody: A succession of sweet musical notes.
‡‡ Joint venture: A deal or agreement between two or more people to do something.
§§ Ammo: This is short for ammunition such as bullets or stones used in war.
¶¶ Clandestinity: The world of spies and spying where secrecy is used to hide from the enemy.

entered the study, Matt Hale's face was serious. *By contrast,*[*]
David Hale was grinning from ear to ear.

---

[*]   By contrast: Instead of; compared to.

8

Practice Makes Perfect

Matt Hale opened the door of his Mercedes sedan and got into the driver's seat. He directed David, who was followed by Thor, to ride in the rear, with the right rear window rolled down all the way. "You've done well so far against *stationary** Coke bottles, Son. Now, for a genuine challenge—let's see how well you can hit a target when we're going 20 miles an hour. If you can do it, my first problem tomorrow night might be solved."

The Hale car started down a long winding road that led off into the farm country several miles from the castle. David felt the breeze coming in the window and streaming past his face. It was somewhat cool this June afternoon and, ordinarily, he might have felt chilled. But, right then, he felt more alive than ever. The coolness of the day seemed absolutely perfect. After all, he was *on fire*[†]—as never before.

The sack of old chestnuts lay on the floor between his feet. His newest slingshot rested in his lap. *Committed*[‡] to following the Boy Scout motto—'Be Prepared'—he had placed a second slingshot on the seat. David was more than ready for the *trial run.*[§] He had been thinking ahead like a good chess player— very much like a good spy.

---

* Stationary: Not moving; staying in one place.
† On fire: Feeling wonderfully energetic, alive and well.
‡ Committed: Having his mind set on doing something.
§ Trial run: A test to see whether a plan will work.

Thor, meanwhile, was doing what dogs naturally do—he was trying to push his way past David to get his snout through the open window. He loved the many smells that came to him as the family car moved *briskly** past farms in the area. Needing that window to himself, David reached over and rolled the left window down for Thor. Now, each could do what he did best—the junior spy could target practice and the Patrol Dog could happily sniff the *aromas*† of the Austrian countryside.

Dr. Matt Hale pulled the car over to the side and came to a stop at a bend in the road. He selected a bush some hundred feet from the road and told David that the bush would be his target area in this practice session. The plan, he explained, was to have David sling one chestnut toward the bush as he rode past in the car. Matt Hale told David that his *objective*‡ was not merely to hit the bush—it would actually be harder than that. The goal was to have the chestnut hit the ground so that it would come to rest just before the bush. In that way, a message could be delivered to Dr. Kaminski who said he would be waiting in a specific spot for contact from the Americans.

They began their practice runs at ten miles an hour. If that worked out, Matt Hale explained, he would increase to the *mandatory*§ driving speed for the next evening's operation. Twenty miles an hour was his normal driving speed in the Russian Sector of Austria. He knew that if he slowed down to give David a better shot, it could be noticed by the ever-watchful Russians. They sometimes followed him *aggressively*¶ in one or more cars

---

*   Briskly: Quickly or lively action.
†   Aromas: Smells which are usually pleasant.
‡   Objective: Goal or intended result.
§   Mandatory: Required or absolutely necessary.
¶   Aggressively: In a forceful, active way.

when he drove in their sector of Austria. His goal tomorrow evening was to alert only Dr. Kaminski—certainly not the Russians!

He mentioned to David, another *ground rule** for successful spies—when you are carrying out a secret task, do nothing that appears or seems *out of the ordinary.*[†] Because Matt Hale always drove at 20 MPH[‡] through the Russian Sector, he would drive the same way tomorrow evening—no faster and no slower than normal.

The practice session began. In his first few attempts, David's shots missed the target by a wide margin—as much as thirty feet. He had to get used to shooting the *projectiles*[§] well before the car reached the bush. Why? Because the *forward momentum*[¶] of the car itself caused the chestnuts to leave the vehicle at the car's own forward speed of ten miles an hour—even when David shot straight out the window. After two dozen tries, David got the hang of it. He was able to have chestnuts land and stop near the bush four times *in succession.*[**] His dad was impressed—so far at least.

Then Matt Hale increased the driving speed to twenty miles an hour—David began missing again badly. At the faster speed, shooting turned out to be far more difficult than David had expected. In fact, he found he had to shoot as soon as the bush came into view. If he waited even a *fraction of a second*[††] after

---

*   Ground rule: A basic principle of action.
†   Out of the ordinary: Different from what one usually does.
‡   MPH: Abbreviation or short form for M̲iles P̲er H̲our.
§   Projectiles: The things being sent through the air—in this case the chestnuts.
¶   Forward momentum: The force that keeps a thing moving in one direction.
** In succession: In a row, one after the other.
†† Fraction of a second: Less than a second in time.

spotting the bush, it was too late—he would *overshoot** the target bush and miss again *considerably.*†

This was not going to be easy—nothing at all like shooting at motionless Coke bottles on the garden wall—just as his dad had predicted.

At first, David was frustrated. His dad was counting on him and the youth was afraid to let him down. But with practice things gradually got better. Within another dozen practice runs, he again was able to shoot the chestnut close to the target area—and do so *consistently.*‡ The rescue operation was *falling into place.*§ When the chestnuts landed in the bush zone for the fifth straight time, father, son and Thor headed toward home.

Before taking the road back to the castle, Matt Hale drove into a farm. He bought six large sacks of potatoes that he put in the trunk. He often bought fresh vegetables to take to the refugee camps—never this many potatoes. With the rest of the family gone to the States, David knew the potatoes were not for the family. Maybe, he thought, they have something to do with the operation. His dad had bought a dozen eggs. "These will come in handy tomorrow night," he remarked with no further explanation.

---

*   Overshoot: Shoot too far beyond the target.
†   Considerably: By a large distance or a wide margin.
‡   Consistently: Time after time, repeatedly, over and over.
§   Falling into place: When good things happen that help get a job done successfully.

9

Preparing the Message

It was four o'clock in the afternoon when they pulled up to the castle. Being June, the sun was reaching its *zenith**—but a few more hours of daylight remained. Matt Hale led David out back to the tool shop and put him to work. The rescue mission was set to begin in twenty-eight hours.

Matt Hale had been told that tomorrow evening at eight o'clock *precisely*,[†] Dr. Kaminski would be sitting on an old park bench in the Russian part of the city of Linz. That was a little over one hundred miles drive from Vienna. In 1945, Linz was divided into two zones separated by the Danube River that ran through the middle of the city. On the north side of the river was the Russian Sector—the American Sector was to the south. A bridge with border stations connected Communist-controlled Linz to the free part of the city. Unfortunately for Dr. Kaminski, at least so far, he was stuck on the wrong or Russian side of the Danube in a part of Linz known as Urfahr.

According to his refugee friend, Dr. Kaminski told him that he would sit in the park for fifteen minutes—from 8:00 to 8:15PM—every third night beginning on June 6. He would do this until contacted by someone who could assist his escape,

---

*   Zenith: The highest point in the sky which for the sun occurs on the first day of summer.
†   Precisely: Exactly—not more or less and not before or after.

unless he was arrested by the Russians. The friend said the Polish scientist was praying that the Americans would make contact with him soon. Well, tomorrow night his luck could change. He would indeed be contacted—not as he might expect, but by *airborne delivery** from America's junior spy!

David's first or immediate task this afternoon was to take one of the drier horse chestnuts and drill in it a one-quarter inch *diameter*† tunnel that would be a little over an inch deep. He was told not to drill all the way through the chestnut. The escape message would be rolled up and slipped into the chestnut tunnel. The carving tool he was given to break the tough skin of the nut was an *awl*.‡ Once he had made a tiny hole, he would use a hand drill left behind by the previous castle occupants. He would soon find he was not as naturally *adept*§ at this task as he was at making slingshots.

David punctured the skin of one chestnut, then another. Each time he tore away too much of the chestnut shell—this was more difficult than he *anticipated*.¶ To achieve some stability, David slipped the third chestnut into a *vise*.** Slowly and carefully, he *excavated*†† a narrow *chasm*‡‡ in the chestnut, just as his dad had instructed. After thirty minutes of *painstaking*§§ work, he was just about done.

---

*   Airborne delivery: Through the air, in this instance by slingshot.
†   Diameter: The longest line across a circle, its widest point.
‡   Awl: A hand tool used to punch holes in leather.
§   Adept: Skillful or talented.
¶   Anticipated: Expected or foresaw.
** Vise: A heavy iron tool attached to a work bench and used for holding things steady between the two jaws of the tool.
†† Excavated: Dug out or made hollow by digging a hole.
‡‡ Chasm: An opening shaped like a cave.
§§ Painstaking: Very careful.

David removed the chestnut from the vise and began admiring his own handiwork. Then, holding the chestnut up to the light, he spotted a little of the nut's loose core deep inside the tunnel. Wanting to impress his father with a perfect job, he placed the nut back into the vise and tightened it again.

As he did, he heard a sharp cracking sound. He watched helplessly as his work of art—under the powerful force of the vise—collapsed and split along its surface. In perfect German this time, David grumbled a couple of nasty words.

David had, of course, *violated** and was learning the hard way another important rule for spies—*perfectionism*[†] is a true enemy of success. In other words, once he had accomplished his task and produced a usable chestnut for tomorrow night's operation—he should have stopped messing with it. Now, he had to begin again and was lucky he had *time to spare.*[‡]

As David labored with chestnuts out back in the tool shop, Matt Hale was in the study carefully preparing the written message. He wrote it in German on very thin paper, the kind used by spies. On the first line of the message he wrote this warning, "Swallow this message immediately after reading it." The *water-soluble*[§] paper would instantly *dissolve*[¶] in Kaminski's mouth.

Matt Hale's message contained further guidance for Dr. Kaminski.

---

*   Violated: Broke a rule or did something wrong.
†   Perfectionism: Trying to do things too well, too perfectly and beyond what is needed.
‡   Time to spare: Extra time available to finish the job.
§   Water-soluble: Able to break apart or be dissolved in water.
¶   Dissolve: Become a watery mixture—in this case, one that can be swallowed.

"Walk in a northerly direction on the right hand side of the *Linz Underpass** tonight at eleven o'clock—precisely! If no one is following you, carry your hat in your left hand and I will know it is safe. If no other person or car is in sight, I will stop. I am driving a Mercedes Four Door sedan and will have a boy with me. I will open and get you into the trunk. If I do not get you this evening, I will be back three evenings from now, Nine (9) June, at 10:00 PM (Repeat 10:00 PM). A friend of *Chopin*."†

"Friend of Chopin" was the *safety signal*‡ which Dr. Kaminski had passed through his refugee friend to the Americans—anyone who said he was a "friend of Chopin" would be *trustworthy*.§

When the message was complete, Matt Hale went out to the workshop. He found David putting the finishing touches on chestnut number four. The father examined it carefully and then lit a candle. David assumed it was to see inside the narrow tunnel that David had excavated. Instead, Matt Hale let some of the candle wax drip into the tunnel and harden. "This will keep the chestnut oil from bleeding into the message, Son. It creates a hard wall that will protect the rice paper from getting wet and *disintegrating*¶ before it is read by its *intended recipient***— Dr. Kaminski, of course."

---

*   Linz Underpass: Where a road passes under a bridge in the City of Linz.

†   Chopin: Kaminski is Polish and Friedrich Chopin is the most famous Polish composer.

‡   Safety Signal: Carefully chosen words of action that tells a spy that he is being contacted by the right people, and not the enemy.

§   Trustworthy: Able to be trusted and relied on.

¶   Disintegrating: Falling apart or being damaged.

**   Intended recipient: The person who is supposed to receive something.

Using a pair of *tweezers,** from his medical bag, Matt Hale carefully inserted the rice paper message into the core of the chestnut. Finally, he dripped a cap of brown candle wax over the opening to the chestnut tunnel. This was to make certain that, to any *casual observer,*† the chestnut would appear no different from any other chestnut under the tree. Yet another rule for spies—make the tools of espionage seem as natural and ordinary as possible to avoid *arousing suspicion.*‡

---

* Tweezers: Small metal instrument held between a thumb and finger and used to pick up and hold things too small for the human hand and fingers.
† Casual observer: One who is not looking, but just happens to see the chestnut.
‡ Arousing suspicion: Making people curious.

Margot and Anne Frank

10

Amsterdam Remembered

When David headed upstairs to his bedroom, it was late. In addition to his natural *aversion** to sleep, his young mind was spinning with all that had taken place this day—and what he would face tomorrow. He thought for a while about the *tangible†* parts of the operation—slingshots, horse chestnuts, the Mercedes sedan, potatoes, the secret message, Russian Guards, and the Russian Sector road map his dad had been studying.

He stayed awake longest this night, however, *reflecting‡* on the rescue operation's *intangibles§*—things David could not see, touch or shoot with his slingshot. Never having lived any way but free, he could only *speculate¶* what the Polish scientist must have gone through to get from Poland to Austria on foot and to have been hiding for months from the Russians. This, the boy concluded, was all about a man's freedom.

David's mind flashed back several weeks when the Hale family had passed through *The Netherlands*** on their way to

---

*   Aversion: Very strong dislike or repugnance to something—in this case, sleep.

†   Tangible: Things that can be seen and touched.

‡   Reflecting: Thinking very deeply on something, not just giving it a passing thought.

§   Intangibles: Things that cannot be seen or touched—such as ideas, thoughts and feelings.

¶   Speculate: Imagine or guess.

**   The Netherlands: A small country on the North Sea next to Germany and Belgium; also called Holland.

Vienna. The Hales spent a few days in Amsterdam, the capital city, where Dr. Hale met with international doctors and nurses to discuss the problems he would be facing in the refugee camps.

While there a family friend—like Matt Hale, a medical doctor—read the Hales a 1946 Dutch newspaper article titled "A Child's Voice." It told of a special young Jewish girl who, just before the war with Germany ended in 1945, died in the Nazi Bergen-Belsen *Concentration Camp.** Of the hundreds of thousands of such innocent and *tragic*† victims of the Nazis, what made her special was that she left behind a wartime diary— one that many people around Europe were talking about.

The fifteen year old girl—ANNE FRANK—spent two years hiding in an attic as her family tried to escape capture by the Nazis after Germany invaded Holland in May 1940. The invasion took place just days before Anne's eleventh birthday—David's present age. Soon, the Germans began sending Dutch Jews off to concentration camps—at least the Jews they could find. Brave Dutch citizens successfully hid from the Nazis some 16,000 Jews who were able to survive the Nazi *occupation*‡ and the war.

The *time line*§ for Anne Frank's difficult struggle to try to stay alive was brief. She went into hiding with her family in

---

* Concentration camp: A large prison camp where Nazis sent millions of innocent people to work and to die in savage conditions. This included men, women and children who were Jews, political opponents, homosexuals, Gypsies, handicapped people, and Christians opposed to the Nazi government and ideas.

† Tragic: Extremely sad, painful and unnatural.

‡ Occupation: When a foreign enemy invades and takes control over another country.

§ Time line: A listing of important dates and events, in this case in Anne Frank's short life.

July 1942—she was thirteen years old. The Nazis *stormed** their secret hiding place two years later and arrested the whole Frank family—it was then August 1944. Within six months she died a death camp prisoner along with her older sister Margot— young Anne Frank was barely sixteen when she *perished*.†

What struck David the hardest was that the Frank sisters had died from typhus—Dr. Matt Hale's medical specialty. David *pondered*‡ the sad *irony*§ that the Frank family had purposely moved in the 1930s to Amsterdam to get away from Germany, away from the Nazis, and away from Adolph Hitler. Going to Holland turned out to have been a *disastrous*¶ choice—of the millions of European Jews to die at the hands of the Nazis, the highest percentage in any country were those, like the Franks, who found themselves in Amsterdam in 1940. Despite the several thousand that survived the war, three out of every four such Jews in Holland were killed—seventy-five percent in all!

Adding to the story's tragedy was what happened to the girl's mother, also in the early months of 1945. Edith Frank died at *Auschwitz*,** a *notorious*†† Nazi death camp in Poland built by the Germans to complete their evil and secret plan to murder all of

---

* Stormed: Made a military or police raid on the building where the Franks were in hiding—breaking down doors and aiming guns at these peaceful, innocent and unarmed people.

† Perished: Died in a horrible way from violence or, as in this case, lack of food and medical care.

‡ Pondered: To weigh in the mind carefully and thoroughly.

§ Irony: When something happens or is said that is the opposite of what one would expect.

¶ Disastrous: The worst possible thing that could have happened, in this case resulting in death.

** Auschwitz: A group of death camps in Poland where the Nazis murdered over one million innocent human beings, including woman and children.

†† Notorious: Famous, not for good things but for doing things that are evil.

Europe's Jews. Separated by hundreds of miles from her children—and with no idea where they were imprisoned—Mrs. Frank had saved and hidden food for her daughters. Unable to bring herself to eat that food, Edith Frank died of starvation.

With all these things swirling in his head about the night in Amsterdam, David had a hard time getting to sleep. When he tried to sleep he kept wondering "Oh, God, why couldn't Dad and the American Army or British Army have arrived in time to save them?" As tears fell from his eyes, he thought of Anne as well as her sister and mother—he thought also of just how wonderful his own life had been compared to theirs.

David's mother, especially, had taught him it was a bad thing to hate people—but then and there, he really hated Nazis. For a moment he wished he had been an American soldier in the war. "Too bad I wasn't born ten years earlier," he mused. "Maybe I could have done something—to save a family or save at least someone."

There was no direct link, of course, between the Frank family tragedy and Dr. Kaminski. The Franks lived in The Netherlands in the early 1940s and the Polish scientist was living in Poland and then Austria in 1947. In David's young mind, however, it was *uncomplicated**—he saw all of them as innocent victims of *monstrous*[†] people. In the case of the Franks, it had been German Nazis who took their freedom and then their lives. In Kaminski's case, Russian Communists were trying to take away his freedom for the rest of his life. This *connectivity*[‡]

---

*   Uncomplicated: Clear, direct, plain and uncluttered.
†   Monstrous: Behaving like monsters or savage animals, not decent human beings.
‡   Connectivity: Being closely associated with another person or thing.

made David Hale deeply *committed** to help save at least one innocent person from such capture—Dr. Kaminski would be that person.

To do his part in the rescue, David had to be absolutely certain that his slingshot would work at the *critical moment.*† He promised himself he would do it right.

He felt a sudden need to *reassure*‡ his dad—and maybe even himself. So, he walked downstairs to the study where Matt Hale was examining and measuring distances on the city map of Linz. The boy looked at his dad and, without further discussion, said simply, "Dad, remember Amsterdam and the news article about the young Jewish girls? Well, now I know why you do what you are doing—I really want to help—and I will!" Then he went upstairs and fell into a deep, restful sleep.

---

*   Committed: Totally intending to do something—no matter what!

†   Critical moment: The exact time when it would be most needed.

‡   Reassure: Tell someone that things will work out fine, that things are okay; in this case, that David will do what has to be done to make the rescue operation successful.

11

D-Day*

Date: Thursday, June 6, 1947

The Time: 5:45AM

Just as the sun was coming up the next morning, David arose, fed Thor, skipped breakfast and headed out to the garden. He was determined to test his slingshots to be sure he was equipped tonight with his very best one—and had a good backup, or spare. Within an hour, he broke one of the less *robust*† slingshots he had carved from the branch of a maple tree. It turned out not to be strong enough for the job.

The one he preferred for the night's work was an unfinished slingshot he had been making from ash—the hard wood used in the United States in the *legendary*‡ Louisville Slugger bats used in professional baseball. Ash proved to be harder and more difficult for David to whittle. But, it promised to produce a more *durable*§ slingshot. David would ordinarily

---

* D-Day: The target day for the rescue operation of Dr. Kaminski. The most famous D-Day in history was three years earlier on June 6, 1944 when Allied Troops landed in France to begin the land war against Nazi Germany and that ended World War II in Europe.
† Less robust: Not as strong or well constructed.
‡ Legendary: Famous for a very long time, in some cases for centuries.
§ Durable: Stronger, tougher and longer lasting.

have *procrastinated** some days or even weeks before getting it finished. With Dr. Kaminski's freedom *at stake*,† he was now committed to getting it finished and tested. If he was satisfied by the target shooting results in the garden, he would ask his dad to make additional practice runs in the car that afternoon.

As Matt Hale had taught him weeks earlier, David built his slingshot in three stages. His dad told him to begin by selecting the proper tree branch which, he said, is the *key*‡ part of any good slingshot. "Son, you can always replace or repair the other parts," he advised, "but, if the central handle or *structure*§ is not right, you may as well throw away the *device*¶—in fact, just start over again *from scratch*."**

After a strong storm with high winds had swept through Vienna one weekend back in May, David and his dad—with Thor strolling along—wandered around the castle grounds before heading out to the *Vienna Woods*.†† They were searching for fallen tree branches that might be used to make a new slingshot or two.

Thor, of course, had seemed to think they were out looking for sticks to throw and that he could chase. To keep the

---

*   Procrastinated: To delay or put off doing something which should be done now.

†   At stake: At risk or on the line.

‡   Key: Most important or essential thing.

§   Structure: The main or strongest part that gives the sling its shape and power.

¶   Device: A tool for doing something, in this case slinging a shot a long way.

** From scratch: All over again, from the beginning.

†† Vienna Woods: The famous hilly and forested land in and around Vienna. It stretches over an area that is 27 miles by 13 miles. It has historically been an area for hunting and hiking and for the past 150 years has been preserved to protect its trees, wildlife and flowers.

*rambunctious** dog satisfied, David spent half his time doing just that. Within a couple of hours, they had found several seemingly good branches—*Y-forked*† shape, about a foot long, and at least ¾ of an inch thick. They examined each one to see if it was strong enough and without *blemish*.‡ If a branch had a crack or was rotted in any way, it could not take the stress and would eventually break—possibly at the worst possible time.

Once they had brought all the selected branches into the castle tool shop, David used his *Swiss Army pocket knife*§ to strip the bark from each branch and look for cracks or *imperfections*.⁋ When he found a sturdy branch, he began the second stage— cutting rubber strands that, when stretched, would produce enough power or force to send a rock, metal ball or chestnut flying through the air. From the inner tubes of an old bicycle tire left at the castle by the Germans, he went about cutting two rubber strips—each about a foot long and a half inch wide. *Pre-war*** inner tubes made from *genuine rubber*†† proved to be consistently stronger and last longer than if he used wartime *synthetic rubber*.‡‡

---

* Rambunctious: Out of control excitable behavior.

† Y-forked branch: A part of a branch that forms two smaller branches and looks like the letter Y.

‡ Blemish: Some weakness or imperfection in the wood.

§ Swiss Army Knife: The most famous military knife made since 1870 in Switzerland. It has several tools, including a small and large blade, a can opener, a cork screw, two kinds of screwdrivers and more.

⁋ Imperfections: Things that are wrong and, simply, less than perfect such as worm holes.

** Pre-war: Before 1938 when World War II began in Europe.

†† Genuine rubber: Real or original and made from the rubber plant; not fake or artificial.

‡‡ Synthetic rubber: A material developed in the 1940s by chemists as a substitute for real rubber.

David had learned the hard way to use sharp scissors to cut the strips. Weeks earlier, he tried using his pocket knife to cut the rubber—the blade slipped and almost chopped off the tip of a finger. By the time the bleeding stopped, David had learned another important lesson, for spies or anyone working with his hands—using the correct tools to do a job is both safer and gets better results.

The final step for David was finding and cutting a piece of leather three inches square. It would serve as the pocket or pouch to hold the chestnut while the slingshot was pulled back and released. The source for the leather pouch was an old Army boot. It was so difficult to cut that David had his dad do it so he would avoid any more bleeding fingers. Another good rule for spies—get expert help when you need it! Everyone cannot do everything.

As David was putting on the *finishing touches*,* Matt Hale came into the workshop to see how the boy was doing. The father liked the idea of having a stronger slingshot and agreed it needed to be tested before tonight's operation. "When carrying out an intelligence operation," he said, "no one likes surprises— surprises usually mean something bad will happen—in fact, last-minute surprises are almost never helpful."

Father and son got into the car and left the castle grounds for a final field test with the newest slingshot. They drove out into the country to the same quiet road and target bush they used the previous day. To make the test realistic, the driving speed would be the same as the required *operational speed*†—20 mph.

---

* Finishing touches: The last thing needed to complete a job—in this case, wrapping some strong fishing line around the rubber strands and the wooden structure to give added strength.
† Operational speed: The required driving speed when the airborne delivery will take place.

Fortunately, there were no surprises. After three tries, David was able to get the chestnut to land in the target zone. Matt Hale went through the test ten more times before he was entirely satisfied. Confident now that David could get the chestnut to the target zone with accuracy, Matt Hale headed for home. They still had time to re-examine all materials needed for tonight's mission.

David then got to see his dad in action as a senior spy—Matt Hale reached into his shirt pocket and took out an *operational checklist** he had put together for the rescue operation.

As he handed it to his son, he said, "David, an airplane pilot who wants to live a long life doesn't take his aircraft skyward without going first through a complete *pre-flight*† review or checklist. Well, David, it is the same with intelligence operations. We don't *initiate*‡ this evening's action until we have gone *methodically*§ through the checklist I prepared. Everything must be done correctly—in the right order and at the right time."

Matt Hale started by *thoroughly*ⁱ checking out the Mercedes. He began with the tires and lights to be sure there were no problems there. He checked the gas gauge as well as the oil level. He made certain the car had water in the radiator. He got down on the ground and examined the car underneath from front to back. He had to be certain there was no gas, oil or water leak that could cause problems later in the evening.

---

* Checklist: A careful written listing of things that are needed as well as actions that need to be taken.
† Pre-flight: Taking place before an airplane flight occurs.
‡ Initiate: Start or begin.
§ Methodically: Going step by step through a number of things needed for success.
ⁱ Thoroughly: Completely and without forgetting or leaving anything out.

He then placed the horse chestnut with the message into an empty pocket in his medical bag and put the bag itself on the front passenger seat, so he could reach it later on. Then he had David pretend to be Dr. Kaminski and crawl deep inside the trunk to see how many potato sacks he would need to conceal the Polish scientist. He had bought six—after the test with David inside, he decided he would need only five.

Matt Hale then pulled out, first, the Austrian country map and showed David the road they would be taking to get to the city of Linz which, late in the war, was bombed *intensively** by the Americans. It was Adolph Hitler who selected Linz, his childhood home, to be one of the so-called 'Five Cities of the Fuehrer.'[†] To increase the importance of Linz, he ordered that military equipment factories be *dismantled*[‡] and moved there from other Nazi-occupied areas—especially from Czechoslovakia which is barely twenty miles away. Things did not work out at all as the Fuehrer had intended—by making his home town an important factory center, Hitler in the end made Linz a target for twenty-two large-scale American and British *bombing raids*[§] during the war.

Matt Hale then took out a Linz city map showing the roads that would take the Hales first to the park where Dr. Kaminski would be waiting and then to the Austrian medical buildings they would visit during the evening. Next, he pointed to the

---

*   Intensely: In a repeated, concentrated way.

†   Fuehrer: Leader or guide in German—was the title for Adolph Hitler as head of Nazi Germany.

‡   Dismantled: To be taken apart.

§   Bombing raids: In 1944, hundreds of American and British airplanes dropped bombs on Linz.

Linz Underpass where they would pick up the Polish scientist at 11:00PM—if things went as planned.

The last road of importance on the rescue map, Matt Hale pointed out, led directly from the *pickup point** to the *Nibelungen Bridge†* that crossed from the Russian Sector to the American Sector. The Danube River flows directly under this bridge.

For the Hale father–son spy team, the *stakes* in this operation *were high.‡* It was not only a question of whether they could carry out the rescue successfully. They had to do it without the Russians ever knowing or even suspecting in the future that they had been involved. Otherwise, this rescue operation would be a one-time event and their future spy roles would be over. Secrecy, after all, is at the heart of this special work.

For Dr. Kaminski, the stakes were obviously, and personally, so much higher—he had everything to gain or lose—it all depended on which side of the Danube he would find himself when Austrian clocks struck midnight and the night came to an end. If the Hales managed to get him safely across that bridge, his life would forever be changed—from prisoner to free man. Assuming he did get free, he could then travel to America or anywhere in the *Free World.§* If he did not make it to freedom,

---

* Pickup point: The place where a person is waiting to be picked up by car in a spy operation.

† Nibelungen Bridge: Hitler ordered building this bridge when he arrived in his "home town" of Linz in 1938. It was completed in 1943. The American Army arrived and captured the bridge in 1945, before the German Army was able to blow it up. In 1947, the Russians controlled the eastern half of the bridge and the Americans controlled the western half. The bridge was 400 yards long, or the length of four U.S. football fields.

‡ Stakes were high: There were high risks involved in the operation.

§ Free World: During the Cold War, this meant all the countries not controlled by the Communists.

he would be forced to spend the rest of his life as a prisoner of the Russian Communists.

After having David trace with his finger the entire route they would be taking to and around Linz, Matt Hale suggested they go to the kitchen for a bite to eat—something to give them strength for the evening's work. David finished the bowl of his favorite beef stew that mom had cooked and left for them in the *ice box.**

Finally, his father broke and dropped several eggs into a *thermos bottle.*† He added some milk and a dash of salt. "This *magic potion*‡ will be useful tonight," Matt Hale remarked. When he explained how the potion would be used, David's eyes widened like those of a barn owl. This was a part of the escape operation he would have liked to avoid. But, if that would be needed, he made it clear that he was *fully aboard.*§ This operation was not about David Hale's *short-term*ᵍ comfort or discomfort—it was about the Polish scientist's lifelong freedom.

---

*   Ice box: Before refrigerators, people used ice boxes or cabinets to keep food cold.
†   Thermos bottle: It is a bottle that keeps hot liquids hot and cold liquids cold for a few hours.
‡   Potion: A liquid mixture that usually has some medical or even magical powers.
§   Fully aboard: Totally committed and without any objections or complaints.
ᵍ   Short-term: Not lasting a long time.

12

Entering the Russian Sector

The Date: Saturday, June 7, 1947

The Time: Early afternoon

Matt Hale drove out of Vienna and into Austria's Russian Sector at the usual *checkpoint.** He came to a stop as the Russian Guard approached the car. David felt some anxiety as the Guard inspected dad's *passport*[†] and then the car. Dr. Hale had been through this checkpoint regularly. The Guards knew him *on sight.*[‡]

Tellingly,[§] the Russian paid no attention to David. This *disinterest*[¶] in children would prove helpful in the future—the younger Hale would be able to see and do operational things without getting or attracting the attention an adult would normally receive from the *paranoid*** Russians. His dad told him

---

later this made David "operationally invisible." He became *thereafter** "The Invisible Spy of Vienna!"

The Guard peered into the trunk filled with potatoes and remarked that Dr. Hale was supposed to have an *official permit*[†] to transport food through the Russian Sector. Matt Hale produced the necessary document which the Guard examined. The Russian had to be sure it had the correct date and the required signatures. This process took five minutes—to David, it seemed longer. In this, his first secret operation, time seemed to be moving quite slowly.

Dr. Hale, meanwhile, looked and acted as *cool as a cucumber*.[‡] In time, Dave would develop the ability to stay *cool under pressure*[§]—a good thing too, because nervous spies do not survive. As he crossed into the Russian Sector, David had *embarked*[g] on his career in intelligence—America's youngest spy. There was no turning back. Flashing through his own mind was a simple, logical question—would he stay cool and calm when the operation got heated?

The Hale sedan pulled away from the checkpoint and David felt better. He let out a deep breath of air. His sense of *well-being*[**] was *short-lived*[††]—it came to an *abrupt*[‡‡] end when he noticed a Russian Military car following closely behind. Matt

---

*   Thereafter: From that time on.
†   Official permit: A paper signed by government officials that allowed him to transport potatoes.
‡   Cool as a cucumber: To remain nice and relaxed or cool, not nervous.
§   Cool under pressure: Being able to be calm when difficult things are happening.
g   Embark: Starting out or beginning.
** Sense of well-being: Feeling good and at peace.
†† Short-lived: Lasted a very short time; brief.
‡‡ Abrupt: Sudden.

Hale, of course, had *spied** the Russian car as soon as he drove away from the checkpoint. He was highly pleased that there was only one *surveillance*† vehicle—not two, as *occasionally*‡ was the case. If two surveillance cars were following him this evening, the pickup *phase*§ of the operation would have to be *postponed*¶ to another night. Matt Hale knew he could fool one surveillance team—but maybe not two.

He told David to relax, act normally and not look back as though he were doing anything suspicious. "Keep the slingshot and vacuum bottle out of sight, Son. As we talked about, the more natural you act, the better. We want to make these two Russians relax—to become so completely bored that they lose interest in us and what we are doing. Bored *surveillants*** can be fooled just about every time."

It was now 3:25PM—four hours and thirty-five minutes before the expected *initial contact*†† with Dr. Kaminski.

They drove away from Vienna along the Danube River for almost 100 miles and approached the outskirts of Linz—they were, of course, still on the north or Russian side of the river. The Russian car tailed closely behind. As they approached the park where the scientist said he would be waiting, Matt Hale told David to look for the bench in the northeast corner—just as he had shown him on the map. This was where David would

---

* Spied: Noticed or spotted them.

† Surveillance: Following someone who is doing secret things.

‡ Occasionally: Once in a while, or sometimes.

§ Phase: Part of a plan, in this case the rescue operation.

¶ Postponed: Put off until another time.

** Surveillant: A person who is following another person and trying to discover secrets about that person and what he is doing.

†† Initial contact: The first interaction.

have to launch the secret message, if his dad gave the command to shoot.

"Do you see it, son?"

"Got it, Dad."

The doctor kept moving past the bench and away from the park at 20 miles an hour—all part of his plan to keep the Russian surveillants off Guard.

Thirty minutes later they pulled up in front of an old hospital now serving as an Austrian Government headquarters for *medical relief** programs in the area. Matt Hale went inside. One of the Russian surveillants followed and saw him speaking with Austrian officials and doctors. They were discussing the *dysentery*[†] that was making many refugees sick since spring. Hale examined patient medical records, taking his time while the *sullen*[‡] Russian Secret Policeman waited near the front door.

Keeping his mind on the time, Dr. Hale suddenly got David and returned to his car, started it up, and turned back in the direction of the park. The Russian surveillant who had gone inside was using a toilet. As a result, he was a little late getting back to his own vehicle where his driver was waiting—very impatiently!

By design,[§] Matt Hale and David had drunk no fluids for three hours. The older spy knew that their not having to use a toilet would prove helpful. So, the Russian car with its two

---

*   Relief: Aid given to people, like refugees, who need assistance. Because refugees had left their homes and all of their belongings during the war, they needed help.

†   Dysentery: Being sick in the stomach and intestines, causing diarrhea and loss of fluids.

‡   Sullen: Gloomy and silent, even appearing to be angry.

§   By design: As planned.

*burly** men in the front seat was well behind the Hales' car as Matt Hale had expected and planned. With the Russians far behind, but driving fast to catch up, the Hales' Mercedes again approached the park. Matt and David both *peered*† into the darkening park and spotted Dr. Kaminski seated on the bench. Matt's watch showed 7:59PM and then turned to 8:00PM. *Zero hour*‡ had arrived!

---

* Burly: Big, strong, rough looking.
† Peered: Looked with some difficulty, in this case because it was getting darker as the sun went down.
‡ Zero Hour: The exact moment when a military or spy operation begins.

13

Bull's Eye

The Date: June 7, 1947

Time: 8:00PM

The doctor-spy gave a quick glance backwards through his rear view mirror and *confirmed** that the Russians were not in view. "Get ready son and I will begin the count down, just as we agreed—seven, six, five, four, three, two, one, FIRE!"

David launched the chestnut high in the air in the direction of the park bench and Dr. Kaminski. The Russian car now came into view, but too late to see anything unusual taking place. Too late to see David and his ash wood slingshot go into action. The launch itself had taken less than a half a second. As planned, once the launch was made, neither father nor son had his head turned toward the bench—or even the park itself. Both stared straight ahead as though watching the road.

The Russians, now having caught up, became relaxed again. They did not want to have to report that they had fallen behind. They especially did not want to lose their *prey*.† Their *Officer-in-Charge*‡ would punish them for certain if they even briefly lost

---

* Confirmed: To make sure that something is true.

† Prey: An animal or person that is hunted—in this case, the Hales are being hunted by the Russians.

‡ Officer-in-Charge: The Military or Secret Police Officer who commanded these surveillants.

sight of Hale. The surveillants now felt comfortable—which was exactly how Matt Hale wanted to keep them. It would then be easier to *lull** them *back to sleep†* later in the evening when he had to pick up the scientist—again without being seen.

Dr. Kaminski, meanwhile, had spotted the Hale car and noticed a child's head in the rear window as the sedan pulled past. Then it happened—a brown horse chestnut rolled across the path and came to rest less than thirty-six inches from his feet. Just then, the Russian surveillance car came into view. It was still speeding to catch up with the Hale car which now was departing the area at its normal 20 miles-per-hour speed.

Kaminski sat calmly for a couple of minutes to be certain no one was watching him. He then bent over, seeming to re-tie his boots. In a *graceful motion‡*, he reached out a few inches and picked up the chestnut. He got up and headed out of the park in the direction of his war-damaged apartment building, not far from the center of Linz.

As the old scientist reached the corner of his road, he spot-ted a Russian Red Army truck parked directly in front of his building. He had no way of knowing whether the Russians were there looking for him or only doing a *routine§* check of *identity papers.¶* Dr. Kaminski decided not to take any chances. He

---

*   Lull: Fool them into relaxing.
†   Back to sleep: Not a real sleep—but in a relaxed unwatchful condition.
‡   Graceful motion: Smooth, natural movement that would not attract attention.
§   Routine check: An unscheduled examination or inspection that is conducted without warning.
¶   Identity papers: Documents such as passport, driver's license, birth certificate that prove that a person is who he claims to be or has per-mission to be in a country or cross a border.

stepped into a doorway where he took this strange little horse chestnut out of his pocket and examined it carefully.

Having lived in Poland first under the Nazis, and more recently under the Communists, Dr. Kaminski had learned to think and act in secret ways, too. Feeling the small *defect** in the chestnut's surface, he pressed hard against the nut until the wax cap over David's hidden tunnel fell off. He spotted the paper note inside. He carefully *extracted*[†] the note with the help of a wooden match and read its contents. "Three hours to freedom," he thought. "Three hours to freedom," he prayed.

For a brief moment, tears of joy almost came to his eyes. But that emotion quickly passed. Fear returned as Kaminski's mind got back to reality. He was not free of the Russians—at least not yet! The sight of the Red Army truck had *jarred*[‡] his nerves a bit. Being free, and being close to freedom, are two entirely different things—worlds apart, in fact. It seems that the closer he got to escaping, the more worried Dr. Kaminski was becoming—a natural and normal thing for men in his situation.

The scientist read the note again to be sure he had not missed anything. He rolled it into a ball. He put it in his mouth where it *dissolved*[§] instantly as it turned into a pasty mixture. It had the taste of rice and salt. To Dr. Kaminski, it tasted as wonderful as *strudel*.[¶] It was, after all, his ticket to freedom. He

---

*   Defect: a rough spot or imperfection, in this case where the tunnel was covered by the brown wax.

†   Extracted: Removed or taken out.

‡   Jarred: Shaken or upset.

§   Dissolved: Mixing with a liquid, in this case saliva—or as David would call it, spit.

¶   Strudel: A fruit-filled pastry, usually apple, found in Germany and Austria.

swallowed and left the doorway, turning away from his apartment and away from the Russian search team going through his building. They were inside looking for someone, possibly Kaminski himself—he would never know.

He cut across the corner of the park and walked deliberately under a horse chestnut tree where he let the secret chestnut, the *concealment device*,* slide down the inside of his pant leg and onto the ground. It came to rest among old leaves and worn chestnuts which had been through the cold hard winter and the heavy spring rains. This was one time Kaminski was glad to have holes in his pockets. Anyone watching him, even closely, would not have noticed a thing.

Eight kilometers away, the Hale and Russian cars were moving in the direction of another Austrian medical center where doctor and son would spend the next two hours.

While his dad conducted examinations of typhus patients, David sat in the *lobby*† trying to read an adventure story about the Amazon River. South America is a long way from Austria, David mused. As his mind wandered a bit, he asked himself which was more dangerous, an Anaconda snake on the Amazon or a Russian Secret Policeman along the Danube. At that moment, he concluded, it had to be the Russian!

David Hale continued to turn the pages of the book he thought he was reading. Then, it occurred to him—he had gone on for three full chapters, but could not recall a word. His mind and inner thoughts had remained entirely focused on

---

*   Concealment device: A hiding place used by spies to hold messages or other secret things.

†   Lobby: The usually large entrance area in a building where people wait to make a visit.

tonight's rescue operation—an adventure that was not a thing of *fiction** or *fantasy.*† This was as real as life can get—eleven year old David Hale understood that perfectly well.

As he reflected on the night's events so far, three images flooded the young sleuth's active thoughts—the shot in the park as he released the chestnut toward the target—then, the almost *irresistible*‡ urge to look back and see how it came out— finally, the two *gruesome*§ Russians waiting for Matt Hale's next move and quite ready to capture a Polish scientist who wished only to be free.

David too was unsure what exactly would happen next. His dad had not discussed the rest of the plan in great detail. The boy knew that the pickup was supposed to take place in less than three hours. David wondered how his dad would get Dr. Kaminski secretly into the trunk of their car. The Russians were staying close behind—they could see practically everything the Hales were doing. Well, practically everything.

They had not seen the slingshot or the vacuum bottle resting on the floor of the car. Both were hidden under Thor's blanket. They had not seen his launch of the horse chestnut in the park. David felt better when it *struck him*¶ that the Russians were seeing only what Matt Hale wanted them to see.

"Ha, they think they are in control," David thought, "when, in truth, they are really mere puppets in dad's stage production.

---

* Fiction: A creation of the mind and imagination; an invented story.
† Fantasy: Wild and unrealistic creation of the imagination; a tale of space creatures, for example.
‡ Irresistible: Unable to be avoided.
§ Gruesome: Frightening and fearfully dangerous.
¶ Struck him: Occurred to him, became suddenly clear to him.

Dad is pulling all the strings—they are dancing to his tune!" The boy was suddenly feeling a great deal better.

At 10:30PM, Dr. Hale returned to the reception area and told David that it was time to get going. As the Hale car departed the medical center, this time the Russians were ready. They followed close behind as Hale drove in the direction of the Linz Underpass.

Dr. Matt Hale, like a trained stage actor, switched roles again. He was no longer simply the infectious disease doctor doing medical examinations, treating sick patients and writing reports. He was now the intelligence operative on a secret mission. He had studied the Linz map intensely—he had measured exactly the distances he would travel from point to point. He knew each of the roads as well as the men who had designed and built them.

He also had been studying the Russian driver who Matt Hale expected to play his part in the rescue operation—although not intentionally. Having driven for several hours with the Secret Policeman *in close pursuit*,* Matt Hale had developed a clear understanding of the personal driving habits of the Russian. He could tell that the guy was getting increasingly impatient and probably *anxious*† to get back to Vienna. He figured that was why the Russian was driving so closely behind—which is exactly what Matt Hale needed to mislead him at the right time.

Matt Hale's mind was on the upcoming *maneuver*‡ that he was confident would free him of the Russians for the three or

---

*   In close pursuit: Following closely and aggressively behind.
†   Anxious: A feeling of not being at peace or at ease; worrisome; uncomfortable.
‡   Maneuver: A planned, tricky move designed to gain an advantage.

four minutes he needed to get Kaminski into the trunk unseen. He looked back through his rear view mirror at the Russian driver and whispered, "Stay real close behind us, *Ivan,** stay really close."

---

*   Ivan: Ivan the Terrible was a brutal Russian leader five hundred years ago, and is still remembered for murdering his own son in a rage. To Matt Hale, Russian Secret Policemen were all Ivans of sorts.

14

The Linz Underpass

Just before 11:00PM, the Linz Underpass was *tranquil**—empty of cars or people as the Polish scientist walked into the tunnel from the south. He had not spotted anyone following him, so he held his hat in his left hand, as the rice paper note had instructed.

Meanwhile, four miles away from the pickup spot, Matt Hale got his three minute *window of opportunity*.† He did this by driving *abruptly‡* to the right at a fork in the road where the main highway *veers§* left towards Vienna. 'Ivan' had been following close behind and was right *on his tail*.¶ So, when Matt Hale swung his car to the right, the weary surveillance driver was unable to follow—instead, he found himself heading down the wrong road and with no easy way to turn around.

As the Russian took the time to find a safe place to change directions, Hale was heading *vigorously*** toward the Linz Underpass—slightly increasing his speed to gain precious seconds free of the Russians. He entered the underpass from

---

*   Tranquil: Nice and quiet, peaceful and sleepy.
†   Window of opportunity: A brief period of time in which to get something done—in this case, pick up the scientist without the Russians seeing what is going on.
‡   Abruptly: Suddenly; without notice or warning.
§   Veers: Turns or changes direction slightly.
¶   On his tail: Directly behind and extremely close.
** Vigorously: With lots of energy and power.

the north and spotted Kaminski. Hat in his left hand, the old scientist was walking ever so slowly in Hale's direction. The Russian *chase car** was nowhere in sight.

Matt Hale pulled over to the side and jumped out. He went immediately to the trunk and pulled out the bags of potatoes. Kaminski followed Matt Hale's directions in German and climbed into the trunk as far as he could squeeze. As he helped Kaminski into the trunk, Dr. Hale noticed that the scientist was obviously and seriously *under-nourished.*† "Just skin and bones," Matt Hale thought, "exactly like so many of my refugees."

Hale pushed the potatoes back in and Kaminski was now fully covered and hidden from view. Matt Hale got back into the car and resumed his drive towards the Nibelungen Bridge.

As Hale drove out of the Linz Underpass, the Russian Secret Police car came back into view. The scowling Russians *resumed*‡ their surveillance. They talked about the incident and agreed not to report their *omission*§ at the Russian checkpoint or when they got back to Vienna—that would only get both of them in trouble. "After all," one said, "the American was out of sight only for a couple of minutes."

"After all," the other *rationalized,*⁋ "this guy is only a doctor who treats typhus. He is not one of the American Embassy or

---

*   Chase car: The surveillance vehicle that was closely following behind.

†   Under-nourished: Being much too thin due to lack of food, and dangerously so.

‡   Resumed: Began again.

§   Omission: A mistake or failure involving leaving something out or skipping something.

⁋   Rationalized: Using reasons to support their conclusion—in this case, faulty reasons that they should not report losing Matt Hale for five minutes.

Military spies we have to watch every second. My guess is he was weary, got lost for a moment, and made that crazy turn. You report nothing when we get back to Vienna and neither will I. Agreed, *Comrade*?"*

"Agreed!"

When they saw that the Hale Mercedes was approaching the bridge leading only to the American Sector of Linz, the Russian surveillants turned their car around. They were glad their work was over for the day—especially since they had a hundred mile drive back to Vienna. They chatted about what a waste of their time it had been. "Why they have us follow a doctor and his kid around Austria makes no sense at all," one remarked.

"What kid?" asked the driver?

Yes, David really could be operationally invisible!

---

*   Comrade: A Communist term meaning ally or friend. The Russian word is Tovarich.

15

Checkpoint Diversion*

Meanwhile, Matt Hale pulled up to the Russian checkpoint. He got out of the Mercedes and headed towards the Russian Guard shack. David stared down at the vacuum bottle at his feet. He lifted up the *concoction*,[†] held his nose, and quickly swallowed the whole solution.

And, just as quickly, he switched his thoughts from stomach to baseball—musing about the Red Sox and Yankees. He wondered whether, in 1947, the Sox might repeat last year's victory in winning the American League Pennant for the first time since 1918. His heart said Red Sox—his brain said Yankees! As things developed in September, his brain would prove correct.

To David, the voices coming from the Guard shack were *incomprehensible*.[‡] He tried to understand what was being said. He wished he had been a better student of German, which his father was speaking. The Russian Guard Officer was speaking a mixture of Russian and very poor German.

In fact, Matt Hale understood all that the Russian was saying and trying to say in his own language. Hale spoke Russian *fluently*[§] although he never let the Russians in Austria know. He

---

* Diversion: An action meant to confuse or fool another person by taking their eye or mind away from the business at hand.
† Concoction: A weird mixture of things—in this case, raw eggs and milk.
‡ Incomprehensible: Could not be heard clearly.
§ Fluently: Just like a Russian would speak.

preferred they assume he had no idea what they were talking about—this gave him an advantage in his medical work but, especially, now in spy operations.

If the Russians knew, or even suspected, that he spoke and understood their language, they would start looking at him quite differently. To begin with, medical doctor or not, they would assume immediately that he might be an intelligence officer. The Russians would take some practical steps, *for starters.**

They would double the number of surveillance teams they had following him around Vienna as well as in the Russian Sector. They would start *recording*† his comings and goings very *thoroughly*‡—in the same way they were already doing for the American Military and Embassy Officers. In other words, rather than view or think of Matt Hale as 'probably not a spy,' they would think of him as 'MOST PROBABLY A SPY.' In sum, Matt Hale could listen in on Russians and understand what they were saying—but he had to be careful to speak to them only in English or German. Such was the care he had to take to protect his cover and protect his intelligence operations.

David, meanwhile, was feeling the *effects*§ of the potion. The internal changes involved three organs—his stomach, his lungs and his brain. Naturally, he felt a great deal of *increased activity*¶ in his stomach. He was also beginning to breathe more deeply. Finally, he started feeling *woozy.***

---

*   For starters: To begin with.
†   Recording: Writing down in a careful and systematic way when and where he was going when he entered the Russian Sector.
‡   Thoroughly: Completely.
§   Effects: What happens as a result of some cause, in this case the "magic potion?"
¶   Increased activity: More things going on at once than before.
** Woozy: Sickish and confused.

He was determined, however, not to let the potion control him or the situation. The young spy thought of the 'guest' in the trunk and covered with sacks of potatoes—an older man who was probably trying to breathe as quietly as humanly possible. "I absolutely will not do it!" David whispered to himself, "not until the time is exactly right—as Dad said."

Dr. Kaminski and David had spoken not a word to each other back there in the Linz Underpass. However, as the scientist approached the car, he had glanced into the back seat and given David a wonderful grin and a wink of the eye. It had reminded the boy of Grandfather Hale—he liked the man instantly.

The voices from the Guard shack suddenly got louder and David's mind got back to his work. He was paying close attention as he never had before. He had noticed, when observing adults, that their voices get louder when they are about to end a conversation—whether on the telephone, in a meeting, or completing official business in a Guard shack. Sure enough, Matt Hale and the Guard *emerged** from the shack and moved in the direction of the Hale car—towards the *secret cargo*[†] hidden in the trunk. Young David Hale, of course, had a part in his dad's stage play this night—he was in the back seat and ready with a surprise *distraction*[‡] of his own.

As the two men approached the sedan, David got ready to do his special part in the rescue plan. His dad was walking in front—behind him was the Russian Guard with his rifle clearly

---

*   Emerged: To come out from.

†   Cargo: A shipment, in this case the Polish scientist.

‡   Distraction: Used by magicians, it gets a person to look in the wrong direction at a key time.

in view. Matt Hale gave David a slight nod and that *reassuring look** that seemed to say, "You can do it, Son—we're partners in this."

The Guard came nearer to the car—no smile, no hello, and none of the pleasant greeting adults usually give youngsters when they meet. "These Russians are *sour pusses,*†" David thought.

The youth lowered the car window slowly. The Guard was now five feet away. "Wait until you can see the whites of his eyes,"—the order given at *Breed's Hill*‡ in the American Revolutionary War—was Matt Hale's way of describing the timing of the 'shot.' David waited, lowered the window further—the Guard was coming ever closer.

The boy was now leaning slightly out the window and this narrowed the gap to a mere three feet between boy spy and Russian Guard. The boy turned away for half a second and put his index finger deep into his mouth. His finger went past the tongue to the back wall where his tonsils once were—before his *tonsillectomy.*§ His finger found the *soft palate,*⁋ as his father called it, and the boy knew something was about to happen. He turned back towards the clueless Guard.

From that point on, everything progressed in what appeared to David to be ultra-slow motion—even the Guard seemed to be moving at a *snail's pace.*** Also, things now seemed to be

---

*   Reassuring look: A facial expression that conveys or gives confidence.

†   Sour pusses: Gloomy people with a grouchy look on their faces.

‡   Breed's Hill: A small hill just north of Boston where an early battle of the Revolutionary War took place.

§   Tonsillectomy: A surgical operation to remove infected tonsils in the throat.

⁋   Soft palate: The soft roof of the mouth in the back.

**   Snail's pace: The speed of a small snail which is very slow indeed.

happening to David without his even trying. From a medical standpoint, David's *autonomic nervous system** completely took over.

David gagged once, and then again. The potion started its ascent. David thought of *Mount Vesuvius*†—and of his own internal *eruption*‡ as milk, egg whites, egg yolks and particles of beef stew exited the stomach in a sudden explosion. The mess exited his mouth and sailed through the air like a *Ted Williams*§ home run. The vomit, which David called "the puke," hit the Guard in the chest—right on the buttons with the Red Stars.⁋ The mess dripped quickly down the front of the coat, onto the pants, and all over the military boots of the startled Russian.

The *commotion*** was total. The Guard did not immediately *fathom*†† what had just occurred. When he grasped what just happened to him, he screamed at Matt Hale some Russian swears. He pointed the rifle and yelled again, this time in German, "Get this miserable kid out of here before I shoot you both—I have six hours more on Guard Duty and will stink all night because of you!"

There would be no searching of the car trunk that evening.

---

* Autonomic nervous system: Centered in the brain, this is what keeps a person breathing when he is sound asleep, or the heart beating, or any other important action that happens in our bodies without our having to think about it or make decision.

† Mount Vesuvius: The volcano in Italy that exploded and buried the Roman City of Pompeii.

‡ Eruption: Explosion of a mountain volcano.

§ Ted Williams: A great baseball hitter for David's favorite team, the Boston Red Sox, and who batted .406 in 1941 before going off to fight as a U.S. Marine Corps pilot in World War II.

⁋ Red Stars: The symbol of the Russian Army.

** Commotion: A loud, confusing situation.

†† Fathom: To understand something deeply and completely.

The 'potato man' would make it to safety. Matt's plan had worked. David too had hit a home run.

When he drove away from the checkpoint, Matt Hale banged three times on the floor boards—a signal that let Dr. Kaminski know that he was finally safe. Buried behind a wall of potatoes, the Polish scientist closed his eyes and said a private prayer of thanks. To all three occupants of the Hale car, the drive across the Nibelungen Bridge was one of pure *jubilation*.* Matt Hale smiled at David and said "Well done, Son." The junior spy responded, "Thanks Dad. But, next time, maybe you will think of something else—I'm afraid I have eaten my last eggs for quite a long while."

---

*   Jubilation: Complete joy, happiness and celebration.

16

Polish Farewell

The Date: June 8, 1947

The Hales' Mercedes headed for a meeting that had been *pre-arranged*** with the 'Midnight Visitor.' It was just west of Linz in a place that would provide maximum protection to Dr. Kaminski. Just because they had succeeded in getting him out of the Russian Sector did not mean that security arrangements would *diminish.*[†]

The Russians were kidnapping innocent people from all Sectors of Austria with *regularity.*[‡] The kidnappers sometimes wore stolen American Military Uniforms when doing their dirty work. At times, they even *recruited*[§] American Military Policemen to kidnap people for them—a crime for which some American soldiers were arrested, kicked out of the U.S Army, and sent to the military prison at *Fort Leavenworth, Kansas.*[¶]

By the time a kidnapped person realized he had not been arrested by the Americans, it was too late. The Russians had

---

* Pre-arranged: Agreed to ahead of time.
† Diminish: Become less strict or serious.
‡ Regularity: Happening quite often.
§ Recruited: To get someone to join the Military, work secretly for an intelligence organization, or become an agent for the Secret Police—in this case, the Russians.
¶ Fort Leavenworth in Kansas is where the Army has its most important Military Prison.

him. If it turned out that the kidnapped person was the one the Russian Secret Police were really after, he would be sent to Russia for life—forever! When the Russians made a mistake and found out they had kidnapped the wrong person, at times they would simply release him and at times they would drown him in the Danube. In any case, it would be *foolhardy** not to continue taking all available security *precautions†* to protect a brave man like Dr. Kaminski until he was safely out of Austria.

Matt Hale drove into a U.S. Army Base that, during the war, had been an airbase of the German Air Force. The Americans renamed it Camp McCauley. He pulled the car into an airplane hangar‡ in a quiet part of the base. The large hangar doors were closed behind them. No one outside could see who was inside the car or who got out.

Waiting in the hangar to greet Dr. Kaminski was 'Visitor.' To David, 'Visitor' appeared even bigger and more powerful than the night he was seen running in the castle garden towards the river. He gave David a nice greeting and got *down to business§* with Matt Hale. They pulled the potato sacks from the trunk and helped the Polish scientist get out of the car and onto his feet. He had been tightly squeezed deep in the trunk for well over an hour— he *emerged,¶* however, with a wonderful smile on his face.

The first thing he did was nod his head in a respectful way to Dr. Hale and then to 'Visitor,' who later introduced himself

---

* Foolhardy: A foolish and careless way of acting.

† Precautions: All of the wise security steps needed to be safe.

‡ Hangar: A very large, open spaced building where airplanes are kept or worked on.

§ Got down to business: Turned his attention to his work, which involved Dr. Kaminski.

¶ Emerged: Came out of a hidden place.

as "Walt Perkins." This was not his true name—it was an operational *alias** 'Visitor' was using in this operation only. Using an alias is a *standard*[†] way to protect one's own security as well as other current operations against the Russians in Austria. 'Visitor' was wearing a disguise which, in this case, was a false moustache and some over-sized black rimmed eyeglasses that changed his general appearance.

Dr. Kaminski saved his first handshake for David Hale to whom the scientist owed so much in making possible his escape. Earlier in the evening, he saw the boy's head in the back seat of the sedan. Later, as he sat alone in the park, the secret-message chestnut suddenly came rolling towards his feet. At that point, he knew that this young fellow had done something very special. Dr. Kaminski was grateful and wanted David to know it. He had escaped the Russian Sector with only the clothes on his back and had no gift for the boy—except to express in Polish how grateful he was for what David had done. *"Dziekuje bardzo,"*[‡] he whispered, which means "thank you, very much."

Although the hour was late, a room in the hangar had been prepared with food and hot drinks for the late-night guests. David's stomach was now aching in hunger—he had left his last meal with the Guard at the Russian checkpoint. He was pleased to have a drink and some popular Austrian dessert, *Linzer Torte.*[§]

---

*   Alias: A false name used to protect his security and identity.
†   Standard: Common, usual or ordinary way an intelligence officer works to protect his operations.
‡   Dziekuje bardzo: Pronounced zed-ku-yeh bard-zo, is Polish for "Thank you very much."
§   Linzer Torte: A tasty crumbly pastry usually filled with fruit jam on top and named for the City of Linz.

When he was offered a hot dinner, he *declined** with a bit of a scowl on his face. Matt Hale laughed and explained why David did not accept the hot meal the U.S. Military team had cooked for them—scrambled eggs with chipped beef was the last thing David wanted to eat!

As it was now after midnight, Matt Hale accepted the American Military's offer to stay for the night and sleep in the hangar building. 'Visitor' earlier had *informed*[†] Matt Hale that Dr. Kaminski was well-known to U.S. Intelligence agencies for the underground work he had done—first against the Nazi invaders, and then against the Russian so-called '*liberators*.'[‡]

Kaminski, it turns out, had run a clandestine *network*[§] of programs in the 'Secret University' that the Poles set up after the invading Germans had closed all the schools in Poland in 1940. The Nazi plan was that the Poles—and all other *Slavic*[¶] people of Eastern Europe—would be given almost no education. If Germany won the war, Polish children would go to school only for four years and learn to count to no more than 500. They would not be taught to read at all! The Germans, clearly, were trying to destroy the Polish people and nation.

With the war over and Germany defeated, the situation got much worse for the Poles. It was now Russian Secret Police

---

*   Declined: Said no, or did not accept.

†   Informed: Told or advised.

‡   Liberators: Those who free people from a terrible invader or enemy. It is placed in quotation marks because the Russians called themselves liberators but, in fact, were freeing no one at all.

§   Network: A countrywide system that included many people from many places in Poland.

¶   Slavic people: Besides the Poles, includes the Russians, Ukrainians, Bulgarians, Slovaks, Serbians, Croatians, Slovenes, and Bosnians all of whom total in the hundreds of millions of people.

who were hunting down and arresting leaders of Poland's Secret University system. They did this for the same reason they had murdered tens of thousands of Polish Army Officers and educated Poles in the Katyn Forest *massacre.**

When Dr. Kaminski learned he was being hunted by the Russians, therefore, he had no choice but to leave his beloved homeland. He had been betrayed to the Russian Secret Police by one of their secret informants in Warsaw and was placed on their *Most Wanted List.*†

He was able to get out of Poland by taking and using the identity papers of a Polish worker who had died of typhus. He walked 450 miles from Warsaw, Poland and got as far as Linz, Austria. To reach Austria, he had crossed the whole of Czechoslovakia and had to sneak across two national borders without being captured or shot. What helped him get as far as he did was that, in 1946 when he left, hundreds of thousands of homeless war refugees were still walking *aimlessly*‡ around Eastern Europe. He was able to join the wave of Displaced Persons without being identified and caught by the Russians.

But, even when he got to Austria, he still was not safe—he was stuck inside the Russian Sector. That was when he started trying to contact the Americans—he knew he could not escape without outside *assistance*§. His good fortune was that he met

---

* Massacre: Killing a large number of helpless individuals and doing so with great cruelty.

† Most Wanted List: This includes the names of people most wanted by the police. In the case of the Soviet Russians, a person was usually not on the list because he was a real criminal but, instead, because he did not support the Communist Government.

‡ Aimlessly: Without any real plan, sense of direction, or goal.

§ Assistance: Help or support.

a former student from Poland who was in the same *bind** as Kaminski. The younger man had managed to get only as far as Austria and was trapped too. But, because he was strong and *athletic,*† he decided to try swimming across the Danube—his 'river to freedom' was what he called it. He did it one night during a terrible rain storm when the Russian Border Guards did not have good *visibility*‡ on the river.

After the young Polish patriot got across to the American side, he was *interviewed*§ by U.S. Military Intelligence. That was when they learned from him of Dr. Kaminski's *whereabouts.*⁋ As soon as they knew that this important Polish scientist was living secretly in the Russian Sector of Linz, the operation to rescue him was *set in motion.***

The rescue operation turned out to be a triple success—an operational *hat trick.*†† It happens rarely but, when it does, it is a cause for real *satisfaction.*‡‡ Not only did it get Dr. Kaminski to the West and out of danger of being kidnapped by the Russians. It also got Dr. Matt Hale back in the spy business. This, in turn, had set the stage for young David Hale's entry into the world of secret intelligence operations.

The following morning, the two Hales—senior spy and junior spy—headed for home. They stopped in the city and

---

*   In the same bind: Caught in the same mess or situation.

†   Athletic: In good physical condition because of exercise and sports.

‡   Visibility: The ability to see things clearly, for example, as one would see in bright daylight.

§   Interviewed: Careful questioning of a person.

⁋   Whereabouts: The general location of a person.

**   Set in motion: To get something started, in this case a rescue.

††   Hat Trick: Originally from the game of cricket—and used in ice hockey when a skater scores three goals in a game—a hat trick describes any difficult achievement that happens three times in a single event.

‡‡   Satisfaction: Happiness with a situation or results.

took a ride on Vienna's *Giant Ferris Wheel** that was working again after being badly damaged in the war.

As Matt and David Hale reached the *pinnacle†* of the famous ride some 212 feet in the air, they could see *virtually‡* all of Vienna and across the Danube into the Russian Sector as well. When they got to the top in the final *revolution§* of their ride, David said to his father, "Funny thing, Dad, but from up this high you can't tell the Russian Sector from the rest of Austria—or East from West—or Communism from Freedom."

Matt Hale nodded in agreement and said "That's why America needs spies on the ground, Son. From a distance, important things may appear the same but be entirely different. America's leaders need to know what is really happening around the world."

Father and son drove back into the hills to their castle home. Each felt good about their recent adventure. David, in his memory, would forever keep the smile and grateful handshake of a man whom he had helped live the life of freedom called for in our Declaration of Independence—"All men are created equal—they are *endowed§* by their Creator with certain *inalienable*** rights—among these are Life, Liberty, and the *Pursuit of Happiness.*"††

---

* Vienna Giant Ferris Wheel: In 1947, it was the tallest in the world and called the Riesenrad.
† Pinnacle: The highest point.
‡ Virtually: Almost or nearly.
§ Revolution: The circular motion of the Ferris Wheel.
§ Endowed: To be given or supplied with a gift or gifts.
** Inalienable rights: Rights that are permanent and cannot be taken away.
†† Pursuit of happiness: The right to choose the way you live your life in freedom.

Before this week, these had been mere printed words on a page in David's history book. He had read them but, given his limited *life experience** so far, his understanding of their *significance†* had been limited as well. No longer, however! For the young Hale, the words of America's *Founding Fathers‡* took on human meaning in the person of Dr. Kaminski. David was now a *motivated§* junior spy with one very good success to his credit and looking forward to his next adventure—his next intelligence operation. "Heck," he thought before falling off to *well-deserved¶* sleep that night, "I'd swallow two dozen raw eggs to get one more person to freedom."

---

* Life experience: The full picture of what a person has heard, seen, and done in life so far.

† Significance: What they really mean to a nation and to its people.

‡ Founding Fathers: Thomas Jefferson and the other American patriots who risked their lives for the sake of freedom and expressed their intentions for America in this document.

§ Motivated: Having strong intention and determination to do what was right.

¶ Well-deserved: One that he had earned.

17

H.I.S.S.

The Date: Monday, June 16, 1947—Third week of vacation for David Hale.

The Place: The Castle, Vienna, Austria.

The Time: 6:00AM

David Hale awoke this Monday morning just as the first rays of sunlight slipped through his bedroom window in the southeast corner of the castle. With his summer vacation barely started, he let out a *chuckle** as he *calculated*† that he still had ten weeks before his new school year would begin in early September.

The Hale children did not attend an *ordinary*‡ school. However, their quite-demanding teacher—their mother—kept David and sister Ellie on a strict 180-day *academic*§ program that she ran in the castle library. They used the same books and tests found in New England schools. Mrs. Hale ordered also the new 1947 edition of the Junior Encyclopedia Britannica which

---

*   Chuckle: To laugh inwardly or quietly.
†   Calculated: Figured out in his mind using simple arithmetic.
‡   Ordinary: Regularly or normally found.
§   Academic: The subject matter taught in advanced educational institutions, including Math, Science, Literature, World History, and Foreign Languages.

gave the children excellent *background** information on many hundreds of subjects that came up in class.

Before she married Dr. Hale in the mid-1930s, Margaret Hale taught English and History. Arriving in Vienna, Austria, she decided to teach the children at home rather than send them away to private school. She *drafted*[+] her husband, Dr. Matt Hale, to teach classes in Math, Geography, and Science. His classes were usually taught on Saturday mornings when he was not traveling around the countryside of Eastern Austria doing his medical work. *Characteristically,*[‡] David *bargained*[§] successfully to have Wednesday afternoons off from school. This was to make up for the Saturday classes and, as he claimed, "would give other children a chance to catch up."

Having *negotiated*[¶] the half-day of classes on Wednesdays, David at first felt great—then he had second thoughts and kicked himself for not having been bolder by shooting to get Wednesdays off altogether. After all, he now *reasoned,*[**] under the new arrangement he had just agreed to, Sunday was the only day they had no school. Once his parents and he agreed to the half-day-off deal, he didn't like the *prospects*[++] he had of getting off

---

*   Background: This is the basic or elementary information about a subject and that does not change from month to month; for example, maps of a country, kinds of animals in Africa, names of famous people who helped build a nation—not the kind of thing found in a daily newspaper or on the radio.

†   Drafted: To select someone to do a certain job.

‡   Characteristically: That which is special or noticeable about someone.

§   Bargained: Traded or exchanged; in this case, he traded Saturday morning for Wednesday afternoon.

¶   Negotiated: Bargained or worked out an agreement with others, in this case his parents.

** Reasoned: Thought through carefully.

†† Prospects: The possibility or chances.

Wednesday mornings, too. In all this *dickering*,* Ellie had been no help whatsoever. Unlike David, she liked school—enjoyed classes—heck, she even welcomed homework! "Sometimes I feel like an only child," he *groused*† to his pal Thor, but the German shepherd just responded with a yawn.

Because the castle school had merely two students—*eager*‡ Ellie and *dubious*§ David—there was no way of escaping the teacher's attention. Privately, David and Ellie labeled it the Hale Institute for Suffering *Siblings*"¶—known only to them as HISS. But, in all this HISS business, Ellie was really fooling—David really meant it!

All the order and close *monitoring*** at HISS made young David Hale absolutely *ecstatic*†† when school was finally out for holidays and the summer break. By the end of the school year in late May, he wished he never had to go to school again. "Classrooms were NOT designed for boys," he proclaimed to his Father. "I can hardly stand sitting one hour let alone six hours in a chair," he announced with his usual deep emotion.

Recalling his own boyhood school days—and weather *permitting*‡‡—Dr. Hale conducted some classes out in the woods or in nearby fields, especially when teaching Science and Geography. When teaching Math, he tried to use realistic problems so the children would learn more than just basic

---

* Dickering: Bargaining back and forth, as in "I'll give you this for that."
† Groused: Whiny complaining.
‡ Eager: Enthusiastic and happy to be there.
§ Dubious: Doubtful or unsure he wanted even to be there.
¶ Siblings: Children of the same parents.
** Monitoring: Keeping track of class work and homework done.
†† Ecstatic: Happy and thrilled beyond anything ordinary or normal.
‡‡ Weather permitting: As long as it was not too wet or cold outside.

arithmetic problem solving. He made sure they learned how to read a map, use a *compass** and *slide rule*,† exchange American dollars for Austrian money, locate the stars and planets, and design a strong *arch*‡ or bridge that would not fall down. He too found it *confining*§ to stay inside. He was, therefore, often the first to suggest they go out for a stroll and discuss trees and plants—and bring Thor, who got restless when stuck in the castle library very long.

Dr. Hale made use of the *flora*⁋ and *fauna*** of Austria to teach Ellie and David the *principles*†† of *Taxonomy*‡‡—the scientific *classification*§§ of plants and animals. He used it to illustrate order in the world of living things as found in both the animal and plant kingdoms. David was delighted to learn that Thor had a more impressive scientific name than just 'dog'." A dog's scientific name—*Canis Familiaris*—pleased David enormously when he learned that the awesome wolf is known scientifically as Canis Lupus. "Ha, they really are cousins!" he exclaimed, when he saw how close the dog and wolf are on the Taxonomy charts.

Taxonomy uses Latin—the language of the ancient Roman

---

*   Compass: A tool or device for showing north, south, east, west and to help a traveler during a journey.
†   Slide rule: A device with a ruler and a sliding piece used to multiply and divide and do other mathematical calculations similar to what a computer does today.
‡   Arch: A curved structure over an open space that supports the weight above it such as a ceiling or roof.
§   Confining: Sense of being squeezed in, enclosed or smothered.
⁋   Flora: The plant life in a certain area.
**   Fauna: The animal life in a certain area.
††   Principles: Ordinary accepted rules and beliefs about a subject.
‡‡   Taxonomy: The scientific way animal and plant life are arranged in a highly organized way according to the things that make them alike or different.
§§   Classification: Arrangement of things by the way they are made, shaped, act, or are connected.

Empire and now called a *dead language.** Why dead? Because it is no longer spoken, it never changes. Because it is unchanging, Latin is used by scientists as a common *international⁺* language. Several important languages spoken today are *derived⁺* from Latin—including French, Portuguese, Spanish, Romanian and the language spoken by modern Romans—Italian. The *gypsies§* of Europe speak a *Romance language⁵* called Roma.

David was glad to learn the scientific name of Horse Chestnuts—*Aesculus Hippocastamon*—that wonderful nut that played such a *pivotal** role in helping rescue the Polish scientist, Dr. Kaminski. The Horse Chestnut took on greater significance for David when his dad read to him an entry made in the diary of Anne Frank. The girl who died in a Nazi concentration camp had touched David's heart. She wrote:

Nearly every morning I go to the attic to blow the stuffy air out of my lungs, from my favorite spot on the floor I look up at the blue sky and the bare chestnut tree, on whose branches little raindrops shine, appearing like silver, and at the seagulls and other birds as they glide on the wind.—As long as this exists, I thought, and I may live to see it, this sunshine, the cloudless skies, while this lasts, I cannot be unhappy.⁺⁺

---

*   Dead language: A language no longer spoken and, therefore, does not change over the years.

†   International: Involving more than one country.

‡   Derived: To come from or grow out of something else.

§   Gypsies: People who move around on old wagons and do not stay in one place.

⁵   Romance language: Any of the several languages that have their origin in Latin.

**   Pivotal: Important or central.

†† From the *Diary of Anne Frank*.

To this young Jewish girl hiding from Nazis near the end of World War II, the leafless Horse Chestnut or *Aesculus Hippocastamon* tree behind the house formed part of the winter beauty she treasured in her final two years of life. David never again looked at such a tree, whether it was bursting with *foliage** in summer or entirely *barren†* in winter, without thinking of Annelies Marie Frank, the girl he *regretted‡* being too late to save.

---

*   Foliage: The leaves, buds, flowers and nuts that appear on trees or bushes.
†   Barren: Bare, without leaves or foliage.
‡   Regretted: Was sorry for.

18

Awaiting More Adventure

The whole Frank tragedy had focused his young mind on the existence of genuine evil in the world—in David's view, that of "Nazis back then" and "Russians right now." Where young David was not entirely accurate was in thinking that because the Nazis had lost the war, they were a *thing of the past*.* Within days, right here in Vienna, he would learn *first-hand*† that the 1945 defeat of Hitler's Germany did not mean there were no more Nazis to worry about—no more Nazis to deal with.

In fact in mid-1947, the same *brutes*‡ who had sent millions of innocent families to die in concentration camps during the war right then and with great *stealth*,§ were highly active in both Germany and Austria. In *Vienna* itself, one dangerous Nazi group had hidden a special *cache*¶ of counterfeit money along with travel documents and gold. It was from Vienna that they were *orchestrating*** the escape of top Nazi *war criminals*†† to *sanctuaries*‡‡ in other parts of the world.

---

*   Thing of the past: No longer existing or important.
†   First-hand: Directly and personally.
‡   Brutes: Men who are cruel and behave more like wild beasts than human beings.
§   Stealth: The act of moving and acting in a covert, quiet or sneaky way.
¶   Cache: A hidden treasure of value (pronounced like "cash").
** Orchestrating: Arranging and managing, as when directing and coordinating instruments in an orchestra.
†† War criminals: Evil men who broke the normal rules and practices of war by murdering innocent people who were not fighting or in any army.
‡‡ Sanctuaries: Places of safety where they would be protected.

Now, with David Hale barely three weeks into his summer vacation, this Nazi group was *setting its sights** on the Hale castle which held the keys to their escape. Their only *obstacles*† would be a brave boy and his fearless dog which, *coincidentally*,‡ was a "German" Shepherd, one who served in the U.S. Army and fought the Nazis in the war.

On this bright morning, David was *unaware*§ of what he would soon be facing. He might, after all, get his chance to strike a blow against those who had killed many thousands of innocent people—like the Frank family. This could not bring Anne Frank back to life. But, if he succeeded, it could help David Hale deal with the pain he felt in his *soul*¶ when he thought of her family and other victims of the war.

For an American boy of eleven who had arrived only a few months earlier from the safety of the United States, he had learned already quite a bit about war. After all, as he and his dad drove around Vienna, he saw sections of the city still in ruins from the Allied bombings and the Russian Red Army *artillery*** *barrage*†† during the *Battle of Vienna*.‡‡ Beyond the physical damage one could easily see in the buildings and roads, he knew some of the *human cost*§§ of war—which he learned

---

*   Setting its sights: Planning to approach or attack.

†   Obstacles: Barriers in their way.

‡   Coincidentally: Happening without any plan or decision.

§   Unaware: Not knowing.

¶   Soul: The inner heart, mind, or voice of a person that helps them know what is right or wrong.

**   Artillery: Large guns that shoot big explosive shells many miles.

††   Barrage: A heavy and continuous shooting of big guns during a battle.

‡‡   Battle of Vienna: The Russian Red Army attack on the Austrian capital in early 1945.

§§   Human cost: People killed or wounded.

mainly from stories Dr. Hale told of the *Displaced Persons** in the Austrian camps.

Dr. Hale worked with *refugees†* who came from *war-torn‡* Eastern Europe. These poor people had the *misfortune§* of seeing their countries invaded and *occupied¶* by brutal armies of both the German Nazis and then the Russian Communists. Some of the innocent and *wretched*** victims of war, especially those who came from Poland, had suffered military invasion three times in the course of five years! Many had spent months or years in harsh concentration camps. They had no money or *possessions††* other than the clothes on their backs and shoes on their feet. The *majority‡‡* of the refugees had lost family members and friends in the war itself or, later, in the terror campaigns of the Russian Secret Police.

Well, summer was here, school was out, and David was *resolute§§* to make the most of what he called his short *parole¶¶*

---

* Displaced Persons: Also knows as "DPs" these were people driven out of their homelands and with no place to call home. Millions of them eventually went to live in America, England and other countries where they could have the freedoms people need to live happy lives and raise children.

† Refugees: People driven out of their homelands. Another name for Displaced Persons.

‡ War-torn: Damaged by the battles of war.

§ Misfortune: Very bad luck with poor results or outcome.

¶ Occupied: When an army takes over a city or country after winning a battle or war.

** Wretched: Poor, helpless and suffering people with no way to defend or protect themselves.

†† Possessions: Things people and families own, such as homes and furniture, family photos and clothing.

‡‡ Majority: More than half.

§§ Resolute: Firmly decided.

¶¶ Parole: Usually a release from jail or prison requiring the prisoner to behave and act a certain way.

from HISS. To him, summer vacation had gotten off to a *spectacular** start. Even in his wildest dreams—and young David Hale had a *vivid*[†] imagination—he never would have dreamt he might become involved in the world of spies. A battle between good and evil. A struggle between innocents like Anne Frank and *vicious*[‡] war criminals now hiding in *post-war*[§] Europe—including one such dangerous group within a few miles of the castle itself.

The young Hale had joined the fight and, in helping rescue the Polish scientist, had enjoyed his first *taste of victory*[¶]—*furthermore,*[**] he wanted more of it! Yet, even though he was delighted to have become Dad's junior partner in secret operations, he was becoming increasingly afraid that the adventure might end and never happen again. "That," David thought, "would be the worst possible thing! After all who will help the next Anne Frank or Dr. Kaminski if Dad and I don't?"

So, before he got out of bed this Monday, he lay a while and *reflected*[††] on things. He had no *concrete*[‡‡] plans for the day; nor did he look forward to anything especially important or thrilling. He did not understand the science of his earlier excitement—the *surge of energy*[§§] and life he felt during his first

---

* Spectacular: Fantastic and beyond the ordinary.
† Vivid: Lively, intense, and strong.
‡ Vicious: Evil, brutal, enjoys hurting other people or animals.
§ Post-war: The period of time after a war, in this case right after World War II.
¶ Taste of victory: The feeling one gets when he wins a competition, contest or battle.
** Furthermore: In addition to.
†† Reflected: Thought about deeply.
‡‡ Concrete: Exacting or clear.
§§ Surge of energy: Like lightning, a sudden and strong lively feeling.

spy *caper*.* It had been caused by a rush of *adrenalin*† through his body. That chemical, which the human body produces naturally, had boosted his energy level and made him feel alive, ALIVE, ALIVE! Now, however, with no such excitement or important purpose in sight, he was feeling a little down. He had little enthusiasm for anything else. Ordinary life seemed too *routine*‡—in fact, downright boring!

For the first few days after Dr. Kaminski had been *evacuated*§ safely out of Austria, David awoke each morning hoping, in fact *anticipating*,¶ that his dad would soon need him and his slingshot skills. More than a whole week had passed but, so far, nothing! Then David began practicing more than ever to *perfect*** his shooting skills. He set as his goal to reach a level of skill with the slingshot that might equal that of one of his *legendary*†† heroes, *William Tell*.‡‡

Five hundred years earlier, skill with the *crossbow*§§ had en-abled¶¶ that Swiss patriot to save his son's life when a *wicked****

---

*   Caper: A mystery or spy adventure.
†   Adrenalin: A chemical produced in the body when one needs a boost of energy—as in a fight, dangerous or other exciting event.
‡   Routine: Ordinary, regular and without anything special happening.
§   Spirited: To be carried away secretly without anyone seeing or know-ing—as with ghosts.
¶   Anticipating: Strongly and eagerly expecting.
**   Perfect: To make absolutely correct and excellent.
††   Legendary: So heroic that people will be talking about the person for many years, even centuries.
‡‡   William Tell: A Swiss national hero who was so skilled with the bow and arrow that he was able to shoot an apple off the head of his son from 300 yards away.
§§   Crossbow: A more accurate and powerful weapon than the regular bow and arrow.
¶¶   Enabled: Helped or allowed.
*** Wicked: Deeply evil person who enjoys hurting or killing innocent defenseless people.

official made him shoot an apple off the boy's head. If he missed the apple, both he and his son would be *executed*.* The tale goes on to say that William Tell succeeded—he did it by making a perfect arrow shot that split the apple from over three hundred yards away. After saving his son's life, William Tell eventually helped free Switzerland from the evil foreign rule.

With that heroic *role-model*† in mind, David had practiced with the slingshot several times a day until his arms and hands ached. He wore out two *hand-crafted*‡ slingshots. When Matt Hale took notice of his son's regular presence in the garden, he nodded approvingly at David's display of *diligence*.§ He gave the boy a *crisp*ꟗ *military salute*** that young David found quite pleasing—it made him feel part of Dad's team. Like Robin would be to Batman.

But, David wanted more than membership on a team. What he craved was direct action where he could do something adventurous and make a contribution—another rescue operation would be just fine as far as he was concerned. He wanted things to happen soon to relieve his own itchiness. But, the world obviously turns at its own pace, not always the way David or anyone else may wish. At times, as in any profession, spies just have to be patient. Patience, however, was not one of this eleven year old's *natural virtues*.†† The good news for this Junior Spy was that he would not have to wait too long to get back in the hunt.

---

*   Executed: Killed or put to death.

†   Role-model: Good example.

‡   Hand-crafted: Made by hand and usually of high quality.

§   Diligence: Hard work and determination.

ꟗ   Crisp: Sharp, rapid and well done.

**   Military salute: A hand signal that shows respect to another soldier.

††   Natural Virtues: The good things or permanent qualities of a person's character and life, such as courage, loyalty, honesty, hard work and, of course, patience.

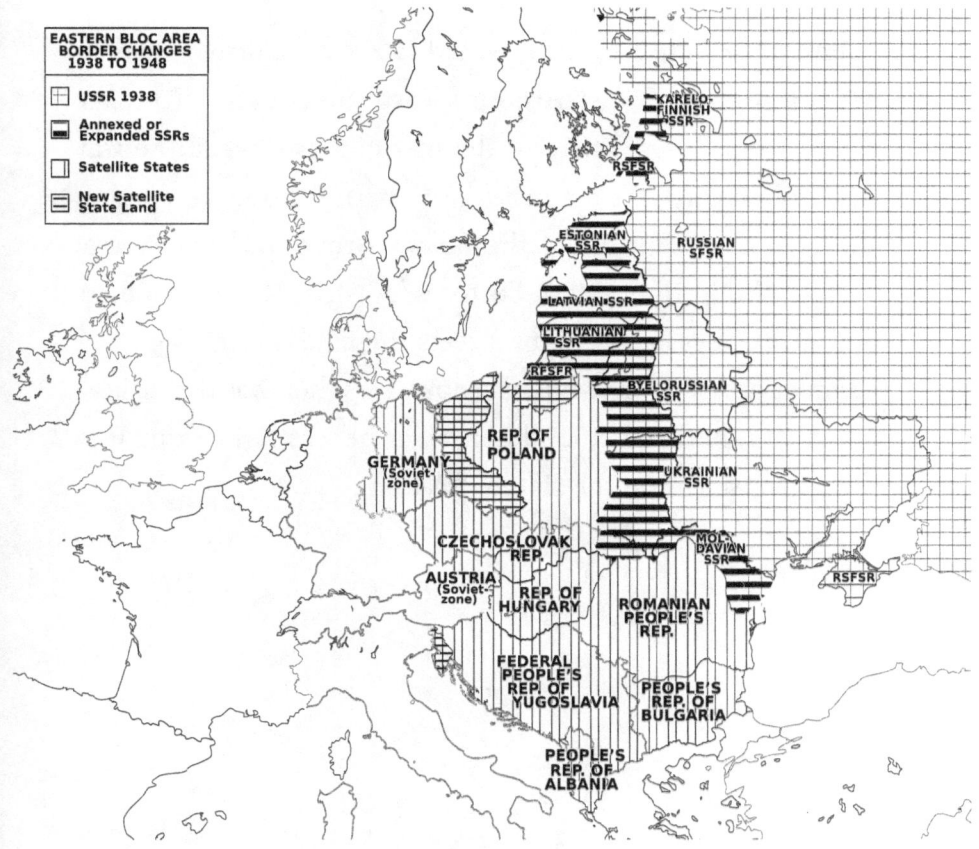

Former Eastern Bloc area border changes between 1938 and 1948.
(https://commons.wikimedia.org/wiki/File:EasternBloc_BorderChange38-48.svg
Author: Mosedschurte, June 1, 2009)

The double tragedy for Austria from 1938 to the late 1940's had come to them first from Nazi Germany to the north and then from Soviet Russia to the east. By the time the Hales had reached Vienna, the Austrians had been through a decade of threats, invasions, bombings and open warfare* not to ignore the loss of several hundred thousand soldiers and civilians who were killed in that period. In sum, both the cities and the

---

*   Open Warfare: A fight were people are actively doing organized violence to each other, as opposed to the "cold" warfare of threats and
maneuvering in secret.

countryside were a mess; it would take over a dozen years to get the Russian Soviet Army to leave the country. To make things worse, everywhere to the east of Austria—all the way to Russia itself—the countries of Eastern Europe were under the guns and controls of the Soviet Army and their Secret Police. Within the Eastern Sector of Austria, Russian soldiers and attack dogs patrolled the streets and fields—night and day, summer or winter, sunshine or snow. This then was the reality* in which David Hale found himself as he was just getting into the spy business on the side of freedom.

---

*   Reality: The actual situation or conditions existing in that time and place.

www.ingramcontent.com/pod-product-compliance
Lightning Source LLC
Chambersburg PA
CBHW050802250626
47155CB00005B/2179